A Place for Our Rain

a Novel

Dennis Michael Burke

To

**Kathleen Butler
and
Beverly Damore**

my sister
and her daughter

⁓

The Hotel St. Michael is in the foreground; the Palace is under the flagpole.

Contents

1. Never Enough Prayers for Girls Like These

Twenty-four-year-old deputy county coroner Antonia Bonaventura walked out from her Prescott, Arizona office a few minutes after sunrise, passed through the courthouse plaza under the city's fresh umbrella of spring leaves and noisy birds, then picked her steps across muddy Montezuma Street, yielding to horsemen and automobiles—the usual red blood cells serving the throb of seven saloons and associated upstairs rooms opposite the courthouse and jail. She stopped for a passing beer wagon full of empty barrels loud as parade drums and negotiated around a blue Chalmers motorcar abandoned but chugging in the middle of the street. From the balcony of a house of pleasure above the Palace Saloon, an Enrico Caruso aria blared suddenly and majestically from the half-visible big horn of a Victrola.

Antonia could not help but translate the lyrics, though she was not in a mood for it.

> *Too early for opera. Una Furtiva Lagrima—*
> *One secret tear. That cathouse is crying for*
> *one of its own—it's in memoriam.*

She stepped high to the concrete sidewalk with the help of an offered rough hand from a passing older rancher she had previously met, made a sideways move through the still-moving louvered doors of the Palace Saloon, then went quickly through the tobacco smoke and noise of that bar, nodding to several weary night-shift bartenders and faro dealers who nodded back. She continued out the back door, across the alley, through the warren of small domiciles used by the hardest-luck prostitutes, finally to Granite Creek.

Under the silver flutter of cottonwoods, three men stood solemnly, talking just above the bubble of the rocky stream. They stood near a body pulled from the water, covered now with a sheet appropriated from one of the laundry carts always queued under the rear stairs of the Hotel St. Michael.

"Mike says it's one of the girls from upstairs at the Palace," the sheriff said to Deputy Coroner Bonaventura as she gathered her skirt and hunched down to peel back the sheet and unbutton the woman's blouse. The men, including the sheriff, his deputy, and Mike Wall, the owner of the Palace, stepped back and turned away in respect. The girl's throat had been cut at a jugular, and a half-dozen knife wounds across her chest were still oozing. Her collared blouse and long dress, once white, were stained by her wounds.

"Oh, I've seen her around. So pretty." Antonia said as she buttoned her back up after formally checking for signs of life. She moved the girl's long auburn hair off her face and stroked her cheek. "A better place, *mia cara*," she said and replaced the sheet.

The sheriff was the first to turn back around.

"This is not what we needed, you know, with Teddy Roosevelt coming to town," he said. "We got to look more respectable than this if we expect to become a state any time soon. We'll keep this out of the papers—the inquest, too, if we even need one."

"Roosevelt's heading to Phoenix, not here," Mike Wall said. "He's going there to christen the dam."

"Well, no, he's coming through here, too. He'll take a quick look at the Rough Rider statue, the mayor says," the sheriff corrected.

"If one of you will keep her company, I'll go fetch a wagon," Antonia said. "And what is her name? Is there a suspect?"

"Mike here says her name is Agnes Bailey," the sheriff said.

Antonia looked surprised. "Say again—first name?" she asked.

"Agnes. And her roommate took off earlier this morning—nobody can find her. He says they did have some pretty good screaming matches from time to time, so I guess she's our suspect—probably another jealous argument over a customer or what have you," the sheriff said as if bored.

"Where's your boss?" he asked Antonia.

She looked up at the sheriff and his belly.

"Sam's in an early meeting at Fort Whipple. He'll be back soon," she said.

"Pretty nice job you landed," the sheriff said. "I mean for a Mexican gal. Very progressive, I guess. I suppose you want to vote, too."

Antonia Bonaventura smiled stiffly.

"What do you think, Mike?" the sheriff asked of Wall, who was standing with his thumbs in his vest pockets. His big shovel of a boyish face was still unshaven, though his black hair was slicked back with precision in the fashion of prosperous men. His lack of beard or mustache always made him stand out and look younger than his thirty-five years—his large chin needed no addition. His shoulders were the biggest of the three men, having needed considerable strength to manage a bar in cowboy country.

"First off, I don't think it was likely her roommate who killed her," Wall said in a whisper, giving respect to the victim. "They did argue because I think they were looking out for each other and didn't approve of their choices. I am quite sure that Elsie Cork—and that's the roommate's name—would never hurt Agnes, or a fly, for that matter."

"You're a soft touch for these gals," the sheriff replied, "but she took off like a bunny rabbit, didn't she? So maybe that tells us what we need to know."

"Maybe," Wall answered. "Or she just got real upset and bolted. It was me who told her that Agnes was dead, and I think she was as shocked as anybody. Anyway, I guess we'll see."

"How tall is she—the missing roommate?" Antonia asked of Wall.

"Five-two or three," he said.

Wall stayed behind with Antonia and the fallen Agnes Bailey as the sheriff and his deputy left. The deputy, thin and young, hadn't said a word. The rumor was that he was the sheriff's off-the-record son, as the sheriff had hired him only after every business in town had let him go after only a few days.

"Why didn't you tell our dumb-as-an-ass sheriff that you come from Italy?" Wall said.

"I guess I don't care enough about him to set him straight," she replied.

"Anyway, yes, my parents came from Sicily. I was born in Frisco. And anyway, there's nothing wrong with folks from Mexico. They stole this land fair and square before we stole it from them, you know."

"I know that. Where's Sicily? I would have bet ten bucks you were Italian. I heard you singing in Italian once when you were drinking with that Italian gal I used to have behind the bar."

"Gina, yes. She was wonderful. She was a teacher back in Italy, but nobody here probably knew that. Anyway, Sicily is in Italy—sort of the Mexican part."

"Well, there you have it. Anyway, you look nice today, whatever you are. You always look real nice."

She was wearing a white shirt with a high, stiff collar and a squared-off maroon necktie that went three-quarters down to her black belt. Her skirt was charcoal and narrow with a muddy hem touching the toes of high-laced shoes.

"If you don't mind, then?" Antonia asked, gesturing to the body.

"I'll keep her company," Wall said. "I'll tell you what, she was a sweetie. She was a sweet gal. She come here not two months ago from Buffalo, where she said she had a no-good common-law husband. Maybe he came here and killed her. Maybe that's something for you to look at, Antonia. You seemed surprised at her name."

"I like the name is all. I knew someone by the name. And thanks for calling me Antonia. You're the only one around here who doesn't call me Tony, which is my father's name."

"Well, Antonia is a pretty name. I like saying it. Do you mind? Me calling you that don't make you feel foreign or something?"

"No. It doesn't make me feel foreign."

"Okay. I'll keep watch here, while you fetch what you need to fetch. Does Sam need to come here to declare her dead before she gets moved?"

"No, I've done that just now, and I'll write it up. I have the authority. But he'll look over everything and sign it, too."

"Well, sure. Not much doubt about how she died, poor girl."

"Mike, do you know her roommate?"

"Elsie Cork. You bet. I've known her five years or so. She comes and goes a bit. A tougher sort, but nice when you treat her right. I never saw her act jealous or mean. I can't figure it was her, but it's a bit strange she took off. I think the two girls were very close, with Elsie giving her the big-sister treatment, like what kind of fella to watch out for and how to be sure and get a drunk cowboy's money in advance. But they did argue like sisters, and I should know because I got six of them."

"I'll have to try and find her for the inquest," Antonia said.

"Be careful, Antonia. Anyhow, you will need some luck finding Elsie Cork. These girls pop in and out of town, you know, and she may have popped out for her own good. Whoever did this brutal thing is not the regular sort. This is not a robbery or a knifing, you know."

"Can you describe her—Elsie?"

"I'm not good at guessing women's ages, but maybe almost thirty, long black hair in two thickish braids, a tan complexion, and, like I said, somewhere around five-two or three. I'm not sure about her eyes, but I think I'd remember blue or green like yours because I'm partial, and I don't think they're real dark, which is, you know, dramatic and easy to remember, or gray, which I think is mystical, so let's say brownish—and big. They're very big, and she has the right nose to hold them up. Good figure. Spectacular caboose if you don't mind my saying. Very pretty in her way. Something of a Boston-Irish accent when she wants it: *Would ya be buyin' a garl a drink?* She talks like that just for fun sometimes. Anyway, Antonia, she's tough from the hard road like poor Agnes here and the rest of the lot with grandmothers praying for them back somewhere."

"Not hard enough—never enough prayers for girls like these," Antonia said.

"I hesitate to mention, and do keep it to yourself," Wall added, moving closer to Antonia and surprising her with whiskey breath so early in the day, "but I think either Elsie's father or mother may not have been white. Maybe from India or somewhere like that, or even American Indian. Maybe negro. Something. I would never ask her about it, but I did hear a customer or two in the bar ask her about her race. She would make a joke about being Black Irish and go into her made-up Irish brogue, and that always got her by.

"Of course—and you likely know this, Antonia— Black Irish is just about black hair on an Irishman instead of the red, not about their skin. My mother said I was Black Irish. She said that when I was about four years old and I started to cry, but she said that it was just a hair color thing—that the Spanish sailors of the Spanish Armada, sunk by the British, made it to Ireland and had babies there.

"But Elsie's claim to be Black Irish was smart, as everyone around here has heard the term, but nobody knows what it means. Elsie might not have been able to rent a room or sit in a decent restaurant in this town otherwise—people being, you know.

"Her name sounds Irish, too," Wall continued, "and I expect she made it up for that purpose and she likes to be called by both her first name and last, probably for the Irish effect. But anyway, since you'll be looking to spot her, I'm telling you all this. Elsie ain't real dark, but she ain't Lillie Langtry either— kinda olivey like you, but you're lighter, and you got a smile on you that's pretty special."

Antonia ignored the compliment, such as it was. She made the sign of the cross over Agnes Bailey and started back to the courthouse through the Palace shortcut, feeling the venerable saloon's history of self-assuagement as if it were an organ of the male body particularly poisonous to women. She then again crossed muddy Montezuma Street.

> *Torn up so much you can't tell it was ever paved. Poor girl. To see a knife coming at you. Even the prick of a rose hurts like hell. I hope she fainted. No autopsy. Spare her the indignity. Cut enough.*

There was the usual gaggle of people in the plaza looking up at the several-year-old equestrian statue—

the pride of Prescott—to honor the Rough Riders who fought and died in the Spanish War. The sculptor of the big bronze was famous all the way to Paris, and the statue was already considered one of the world's finest of the equestrian sort—this according to Mike Wall, who had given her a tour of the town when she first arrived. Nearly every Prescottonian had worked hard one way or another to raise the $10,000 to fund it, he said. Women raffled cakes, children sold lemonade, and business owners competed in their generosity.

He was proud that the whole commercial side of Montezuma Street, including the Palace and the St. Michael, all of which had burned to the ground in 1900, was now fancier than ever. He was particularly proud that the Palace's half-drunk patrons had somehow lugged the mammoth carved back bar across to the plaza to save it from the fire.

"It had come a long way by sea around the Horn, then by steamer up the Colorado River, and then by ox wagon through dangerous Mojave lands," Wall had said.

Antonia challenged that:

"I was told the Mojave are a peaceful, farming people," she said.

"Well, they are when they are," he replied. "Mostly because that's what the U.S. Government and the Army tell them to be, but every now and then one of their kwanamis—that's their name for a brave warrior—decides to go do something. So, you still got to be careful through there."

"Kwanamis?—do you know their language?" She asked.

"Only a few words—mostly greetings. I did some business with them before I got into the bar business. I like them. They are big on dreams and such. They say you can dream yourself back to the creation. When a big telescope was put up in Flagstaff, they sent some elders to go take a look through it to see what they could see of creation. They called the telescope fellows the 'men with long eyes.' I admire their curiosity."

She was thinking of Wall as she crossed the plaza but then admonished herself for being so callous as to not be concentrating on the brutal killing. She was not surprised that the young woman's murder had not upset the street. Mozart's Requiem in D minor was playing now from the balcony Victrola, but no one paid notice. A dead prostitute was not something polite people would mention anyway, perhaps for fear of causing trouble for some too-energetic brother of their own fraternal order.

She and Yavapai County Chief Coroner Sam Dill examined the corpse while it was still in the Ruffner Mortuary wagon. Dill then looked over Antonia's handwritten report and signed it. Other than bruises and knife wounds, the only evidence found, and by Antonia, was a hair that clearly did not belong to the victim.

"I'd like to try to go find the girl's roommate for the inquest," Antonia said to Dill. "She's on the run."

"Well, that's fine. That's a fine idea. Take as long as you like. I'll give you two days and a budget of fifty dollars."

He handed her a $50 gold slug from his own pocket. She figured it came from a faro table in the Palace and that he would bill the county double.

She was used to the idea that Dill didn't have much use for her and had only hired her because he misheard that she was the daughter of a fourth-degree Knight of Columbus, like himself, and he may have thought she would be easier to push around than a male assistant—another misunderstanding.

She had learned her trade in a coroner's office that was made busy by San Francisco's great earthquake, five years earlier. But, as she could not advance in that office without a full medical doctor's degree, she responded to an advertisement from Prescott in a society journal. She missed the sparkling sea and bay and the gilded wealth and the Italian section of San Francisco and its foods, voices, music, theatre, and the constant froth of characters—the children and grandchildren of Forty-Niners who insisted on being as colorful as their forebearers and twice as rich. The city was still partially in ruins when she left, but new life was coming up like grass and aspen after a fire.

Finding the missing saloon girl Elsie Cork would not, she knew, be easy. Such women might change their names with each new town. But at the Prescott train station, Antonia found a ticket agent who remembered a girl of her description who had boarded the Santa Fe train to Phoenix and Maricopa that morning. He said he thought the woman bought a ticket to the end of the line, Maricopa. From there, she could have caught the Southern Pacific to California or eastward to New Orleans and beyond. But he remembered that she had to fish deep into her purse to find enough coins for the ticket, so she might not have been able to go very far.

Antonia knew such a woman could work a few evenings in Maricopa to pay her way from there, and so there was no time to waste in finding her.

At the Palace, she asked Wall if there were any houses of joy in Maricopa. He told her that there would have to be one or two, owing to the railroad there. She went to her rented room on Willis Street and packed her carpetbag, making the 4:40 evening train and wearing the same outfit, sponged off.

She did not favor long periods alone unless she could sleep, and she could not sleep well on the train. The Santa Fe south from Prescott was referred to as *the Peavine*, as it made countless slow twisty turns down the mountains. She dreaded such hours because her memory would take her back to the San Francisco earthquake, which was unbearable if she let herself spin down into its particular hell.

She understood enough of the human body and its brain to know that she needed to build new memories, new ideas, layered over the old. She resolved to think only about the case at hand and fill her brain with it. She was quite certain that the woman being pursued was not the killer. Was it a fool's errand, then? No, she wanted to think about what the woman might tell her. And then what? She was not a sheriff. What would she do with whatever information she might gain?

But the earthquake came back with every jerk of the train. It jiggled the small crystal electric lamps along the ceiling and made castanets of coat buttons and buckles on the bright brass rails of the long overhead racks that gleamed through veils of cigar smoke and disappeared into the gloom at the far end of the car.

The window adjacent to her seat was opened an inch for fresh air, but that let in as much smoke from the wood-burning engine as it let out cigar smoke. The smell of burning wood kept defeating her resolve to not think of the earthquake and its fires.

"Are you all right, miss?" an elderly man asked. She was not aware that she was showing her emotion. In the dark of the car, she could only see his outline and smell pipe smoke on him and wool.

"Thank you very much, sir. I am fine."

"Let me sit here with you, if you don't mind."

The man did so and was soon asleep next to her. She didn't mind that his shoulder slumped slightly against her. A bit of sleep came and a dream of an Easter hunt with children in a place that was variously Golden Gate Park and Heaven.

After a dozen brief stops and a long stop in Phoenix, where the older gentleman patted her shoulder to make sure she did not oversleep her stop and wished her a good evening, she and five others continued on, arriving in Maricopa at midnight.

The little town was so dark that she had to stand for a minute on the platform to let her eyes adjust. A mammoth water tower hovered over the railyard, blocking half the stars. The moon had set but left a glow on the horizon that showed sharp mountains to the northwest.

Daddy wouldn't like me being in this dark place.

The Maricopa Station

2. Women at Breakfast

Antonia spotted a white-haired clerk fluttering inside a stationhouse that seemed to hang in the dark like a green wooden birdcage. She went inside to ask about accommodations.

"Well, ma'am," he said, "we got the Hotel Williams, directly across the tracks there, and also the Edwards, around the corner. They both accommodate ladies, but different sorts, if you know what I mean."

"Which one is for gentlewomen?"

"Either one, ma'am. I shouldn't have made the comment. They both are nice now, but mostly the Williams—the Williams is very nice."

"Thanks. I suppose the Southern Pacific has been through today, east and west, but I'd like to know if either was boarded by an unaccompanied woman of about thirty, darker complexion, normal height and build, and long black hair in two braids."

He cocked his head to think. He said neither train took on a woman of that description, and that he would surely know, as he'd been working two shifts straight, due to his assistant's wife being in labor.

She asked if the woman she had described might have arrived on the train from Prescott in the early afternoon. He said, unless they needed a ticket elsewhere, he didn't normally give attention to the people getting off.

"I heard a piano outside just now. I expect that was from a bar and all that goes with it?" Antonia asked.

"Yes ma'am. There is two bars that rattle on all night, and that's where things happen, if you get my drift. It might not be too smart for you to go into either of those bars, this time of night, particularly."

"I will pay you a dollar if you'll take me in there to have a quick look. A dollar each bar."

"Well, I'm a family man with a wife and all, and this town is smaller than you can imagine when it comes to what the husbands are up to, so I'd have to say no. I don't mean anybody will harm you if you go into those places, but you'll cause a stir, looking the way you do. You'll cause a stir."

"What is wrong with the way I look?"

He cocked his head again, looking at her slightly sideways. "Nothing wrong, ma'am, and there's your problem. Them cowboys in there might think a goat with a fresh bonnet is a fine-enough creature for their attentions. They don't but rarely see pretty things like you up close. But I'm sure you can put your trust in the bartenders, as they keep folks in line."

The piano music was coming from the small bar immediately next to the Hotel Williams. She stood in the doorway long enough to see a woman standing near the end of the bar who fit the description of Elsie Cork.

Antonia backed away and went instead into the Williams. With the half-asleep, unfriendly woman behind the desk, she registered for two rooms—one for herself, the other for Elsie —and then returned to the bar. This time she went inside. The piano music stopped.

"I recognize you," Elsie Cork said to her. They stood together at the splintered bar. "You're that gal deputy sheriff in Prescott."

"I'm no deputy sheriff," she replied. "My work is more in the medical line."

An eavesdropping older man of torn shirt and trousers, like a floppy doll come half to life, limped close to the two: "My sister is a nurse," he said. "I love the nurses. Let me buy you a drink, miss." He was directing his offer to Antonia and clearly away from Elsie.

"Well, I'm not exactly a nurse, sir, but I appreciate that you respect your sister, and I suppose she taught you how to treat a woman properly, as all you need is to think how you want her treated. Am I right?""

The man nodded and backed off, double-crossed by his conscience.

The bartender, as ill-kempt as any other man in the place but younger, raised his caterpillar eyebrows and pointed to the bottles behind him.

"Your sister hasn't bought a thing," he said to Antonia. "Maybe you'll be a better customer."

"We're not sisters, but whiskey please for me and one for my friend," Antonia said, putting down a dollar and motioning Elsie to a table under windows that were nearly painted black with railroad soot. A half-dozen men sat at other tables, all watching. The music, which had come from a player piano, did not resume.

That they might be taken for sisters was understandable to Antonia as she looked at Elsie across the table. For big, dark eyes, Elsie took the ribbon over Antonia's small green ones, but both women shared plump lips and narrow faces, though Elsie's tiny chin made her lips more important to her face. Antonia's light brown hair was above her shoulders in a curly pompadour that would support a big hat if she ever might want one. Elsie's black braids were less stylish but more distinctive. They both had bold eyebrows and hints of dimples, which Antonia saw in Elsie when she smiled bitterly after sitting down:

"Why are you after me?" she said.

"I'm not after you. But I think you can help me find who killed Agnes Bailey, your friend."

"I'm not going to tell you anything, lady. You can arrest me or not arrest me, but that's about it. I don't know a thing, and if I did, I wouldn't tell you. I got my own hide to look after, and that's what I'll do. And maybe you think it was me who killed her? It weren't."

"Miss Cork, I know it wasn't you because you couldn't have managed it. She was killed by someone who held her from behind. Someone big enough to do that and cut her throat and stab her in the chest. Agnes was taller than you, and whoever killed her was taller than her. And I've never seen a woman kill someone that way. The killer was someone who has killed people before, maybe lots of people—he cut her throat in just the right place. I learned my trade in San

Francisco and saw a lot of killing. Also, you're not an older man with a beard."

"What does that mean?"

"It means I found a hair tangled in her hair that does not belong, and it's gray and curly like a beard. It's being held safe in Prescott for the inquest."

"Well, you're right about me; I can't grow a beard worth spit. And if I could, I wouldn't let it go gray."

Antonia placed the two hotel room keys on the sticky, initial-carved table.

"Pick a key. I got you a room for tonight in the hotel next door. You don't need to fuck any of these fellows."

From the men in the room came a mock sigh of disappointment.

"Thank you, I'll take it," Elsie Cork said. "But then what? I don't have enough to get out of Arizona. It's such a tiny town, I'd have to screw everyone twice. And just my luck, I think it's just about my time of the month, and you can only charge so much for the other stuff, as you know—I mean, as you can imagine. Anyway, I'm always glad to see the curse come, not only for the holiday but for the assurance."

"Tomorrow morning," Antonia replied, "you and I will have coffee and some eggs somewhere, and you can decide which direction you want to go, because, if you will tell me everything you know, I'll buy you a day's travel east or west, your choice. If that's not good enough—if you think you're not safe anywhere else, you can stay a few days with my father in San Francisco. Then you could find your own place, and there are never enough saloon girls in Frisco. Your choice. Do we have a deal? If you were any friend to Agnes Bailey, you will want to tell me everything anyway, as I want to catch her killer and I'm probably the only one who cares to."

"It's fine," Elsie said curtly, picking up a key and standing to leave.

"I'm going to knock on your door at seven-thirty," Antonia said. "Be downstairs at eight. Don't sneak away in the night. I'm already feeling… I just would hate... I don't have the money to keep chasing you. Be a friend."

Elsie looked at her for a long moment. Her eyes then flashed, and she made a little laugh and said, "All right. Don't worry," and Antonia figured she meant it.

> *She is Carmen. So much life. Doomed but lovely in her way. I am a child next to her. She should sing her part. The knife that killed her friend is waiting for her.*

In the morning Antonia Bonaventura was surprised by the elegance of Elsie's dress and appearance when she came down to the lobby. They both looked like they could be on their way to church as they walked to the other hotel, the Edwards, for breakfast. The street was nearly empty of bustle, as the town only came alive in the minutes before and after a train arrival. Antonia could see what Mike Wall was talking about regarding Elsie's possible parentage, but she might not have noticed otherwise. There was no challenge to her in the restaurant, and she could see that Elsie's attitude of presumption toward the waitress would have made any challenge unimaginable. Also, they well might be thought sisters, and Elsie's own lighter looks could help average things out.

"I don't want to bother your father," Elsie said, "but the fact that you would let me stay with him—if that was a real offer—makes me think you really do think I'm innocent, which I am. But I would like it if you could sport me the fare to San Francisco. I have some friends of my own there, and you're right about the place being easy business."

"It was a real offer, and I will buy you the ticket if you'll tell me everything you know. I'm going out on a limb here with my job because, in Prescott, they still think you maybe did it, and I'm supposed to find you and bring you back for the inquest. So, some railroad or hotel big mouth is going to let on that I found you and not only let you go but paid your way. That's what I have at stake in this, so make it worth my risk. We have less than an hour before the first train to California comes through. My train back to Prescott is soon after that, and I need to catch that one."

Antonia then halved a side of flapjacks to share.

Elsie Cork heartily and happily feasted on the pancakes, scrambled eggs, bacon, potatoes, and coffee, with a mouth so ever full that Antonia worried the woman might choke to death before telling what she knew. Her attack on the food sometimes made the table rattle, which, through the rough wood floor and papered wood walls, made a high shelf of Blue Willow plates and cups rattle above them.

But Elsie finally set down her silver, dabbed her lips, and began:

"Thank you. I didn't eat yesterday. All right, Agnes was with some rough man the night before she was killed—two nights ago, I guess. She was laughing about how drunk he was, but she was also upset and needed to talk to me to get it out. The man had asked her where she was from, as men do, and she said Buffalo. He wanted to know if she knew Buffalo Joe. She laughed, thinking it was a joke of some kind, but the fellow said, no, he meant Prescott's Buffalo Joe.

"Agnes told him she'd never heard of him. He was, like I said, drunk, and said, well, she should have heard of him because he is a friend of his and he changed U.S. history. When he was putting it in her roughly, he leaned to her ear and whispered that Joe was the fellow who fixed it so McKinley got shot in Buffalo. That's why the nickname. Then he said, 'I guess I shouldn't-a told you that,' and laughed.

"She asked him who McKinley was as if she didn't know. He leaned into her again and said, 'You dumb bitch, he was the president of the U.S. of A.'

"Well, she said nobody ever talked to her like that before, and it made her feel like trash. She was laughing and crying about it. She said she had known very well who McKinley was, especially being from the city where he got killed only ten years before, but she wanted to play dumb because that's generally how you get out of situations with men like that.

"So, next morning, I was working on some men at the bar downstairs for an hour or so and she was supposed to go shopping at the Goldwater store for a corset. They let us shop in there an hour before they open to decent folk. About an hour later I went up to our room to spruce up the place because I wanted to get a fellow up there later. Mike came in and told me they had found her dead. I just sat down and cried and tried to think what to do. I remembered that thing she told me, and now it scared me because people knew we were close, and friends like us talk to each other about everything. So, I packed my bag and just walked down to the station without saying goodbye to anybody. The Peavine was just about to leave, and I caught it. I was a little short for the ticket, so I promised the ticket guy a fuck when I got back. But I'm not going back, so I feel bad about that. Could you square that for me with him?"

"I'm not fucking him."

"No, I mean, could you give him two dollars? His name is Cliff. I'll owe you. I'll repay you someday."

"Okay. And just so you know, the man who killed McKinley was one of those crazy anarchists. It wasn't a cowboy from Prescott," Antonia said as she stabbed a yoke.

"All I know is what Agnes said that he said, and she didn't make things up."

"I'm going to have to look into all that, starting with the fellow who said that to her."

"How will you do that? She didn't even tell me what he looked like—not even old or young. Maybe he was a drunk with a head full of sawdust and made all that up, and someone else killed her?"

"Maybe, but he's all we have for now, and it would be a little too much of a coincidence for her to have two such unusual things happen to her so close. They're very likely related."

"Well, you don't know the life, miss. We have strange things happen ten times a day."

"I'm sure you do," Antonia replied. "Anyway, that drunk will indeed be hard to find. And all we know about the killer is he was bearded or long-curly-haired, and tall, or at least taller than Agnes. I do hate to say this, but her killer might go free, you know. That's a shame. Devil's luck. She deserves better. But the only way to catch him would be for you to go back to Prescott and see if he comes after you—after we spread the word that Agnes told you what he said. But I would never ask you to do that. I think you like your life too much to risk it over a dead friend. There would be no point to it, really. I mean nobody much cared about her in life, and her murder will be forgotten in a week. All anybody cares about right now is that Theodore Roosevelt is coming to Arizona."

There was silence as Antonia's worm wiggled on the hook and the whistle of the arriving Southern Pacific sounded in the distance. Elsie played with the ends of her braids as she thought.

"What do you mean, exactly," she finally bit. "And *of course* you know I cared about her and can see very well what you're doing, miss. You're using me—a whore—with no bother for my life or health, and just so you can say to some Prescott fellows that you done something. That's what cowboys do, miss. You're just sacrificing a pawn. But, okay, I'll do it."

3. Curious Meetings

On the train back, Antonia thought aloud with Elsie. They would arrive up north quite late. The plan was to disembark at the last stop before Prescott, at the summer enclave of Iron Springs, now mostly still deserted until hotter weather. Mike Wall, of the Palace, owned a cabin there that he rarely used; he had taken it in payment for a man's gambling debts. Antonia was always welcome to use it and knew where the key was hidden. The cabin was quite near the train stop, so the plan was for Antonia to open the place up for Elsie and then get back on the train, arriving in Prescott alone.

"When I get back to the coroner's office, I'll tell Dill that you will be staying at the St. Michael and have agreed to be at the inquest to tell everything you know, which has something to do with politics. I'll tell the sheriff and a few others, and they will spread that around because that's what they do. That sets up the bait. I'll get you a room at the St. Michael in your name and you and I will stay there until the inquest. If the killer comes for you, I'll be there. And, after the inquest, there's no further risk to you, because everything you know will be all out in public. But we'll hope the killer shows his hand before then."

"That's the fancy hotel," Elsie replied. "You're spending a lot on me. I expect you have a little gun somewhere in that bag and can protect me, but it's a risk, isn't it—and for you?"

"It is, but you agreed to help, and I think it's less risky than letting you go off alone somewhere, maybe with someone after you, and you being in your present mood."

"What does that mean?"

They were seated in the plush velvet chairs of a club car that was no longer in its prime. With each shift in her chair, Antonia could smell years of tobacco use rising around her. She shifted to get comfortable.

"You were nervous enough to run," she began, "but calm as a cucumber when I found you last night. You had made up your mind that nothing mattered anymore. That's a dangerous place to be, and it's quite a common feeling among people who have been near a sudden and senseless death. And you didn't eat yesterday. You were broke, but any man on the train would have bought you a ham sandwich from the dining car. I could see in your eyes last night the same nothing I saw in so many eyes after the earthquake in Frisco. It often ends poorly."

"The expression is *cool* as a cucumber, not calm, Miss Bonawhatever," Elsie said. "Being calm is not something a cucumber does."

"It's Bonaventura."

The land outside the window was endlessly empty. They were both watching it roll by.

"I know; I know your name," Elsie said without looking away from the expanse outside. "So much world, there is," she said in her Irish impersonation. "Why do we pack our sorry selves into cruel towns?"

Antonia did not hazard a guess.

"I'm going to get you a little sack of sandwiches from the porter, so you won't starve at the cabin," she said instead.

By the time they passed the station at Kirkland Junction, long after a stop in Phoenix of several hours, the stars were beginning to show their glory. Low hills of yellow grass found illumination in the great headlamp of the train as it made its curves.

At Iron Springs, Antonia asked the conductor to please hold the train long enough for her to open a cabin for her friend—she pointed into the dark toward the cabin to suggest that it was very close. He glanced at his pocket watch and agreed to five minutes, as the train was running that much ahead.

"Make it quick as you can, miss," he said. "This stop always worries me, as there are leprechauns here and about, you know."

The man was older and quite short. He spoke with enough Irish that Antonia nearly laughed at what he said, but she held it in, thinking that he was being serious in his way. He tossed down the dented steel stepstool for Antonia and Elsie, then followed them down to the gravel himself, where he scanned the woods with a lantern that did no good for that.

From Mike Wall, Antonia knew the reference and explained it to Elsie as they walked quickly through the dark to the cabin: The Iron Springs stop was in a small depression between two hills. The Iron Springs kids, when they were otherwise bored, greased the tracks with lard stolen from their mothers' kitchens so that the train would have a devil of a time getting uphill from a standing start. Regular passengers on the Peavine were enough used to it to groan in unison when they heard the steam engine's great rods and wheels starting to move, while the view outside the windows remained the same—often of smiling, innocent children.

The drab khaki paint of Mike Wall's cabin made it hard to see in the dark among the pines. Inside, Antonia found a kerosene lantern but no kerosene. They were both standing in darkness except for the light of one safety match at a time, found in a box on the hearth. Elsie then spotted a small switch on the wall near the door.

"It's electrified," she said, pushing one of the two buttons on the little box and illuminating the cabin with a chandelier made of a wagon wheel that had been invisible above them. The bedrooms were electrified, too, and she found one with a made bed and a pitcher of water for washing that seemed full and fresh enough. The mattress was but a few inches thick over a folding steel bed of tin strips and squeaky springs that looked to have once been the property of the U.S. Army.

"I've slept on worse," she said.

The women shook hands and Antonia departed on a run for the train. The conductor had already withdrawn the stepstool, but he gave her a hand up and was, she thought, strong for his size and age.

"I expect you girls got to chatting," he said with a cold stare.

She was in Prescott a half-hour later, a bit before midnight.

In the Coroner's office the next morning, Antonia found Sam Dill sitting at his desk under a popular but inaccurate new poster of cowboy soldiers on horses storming San Juan Hill, flying the newly proposed Arizona flag and trampling Spaniards painted to look considerably less than human. Dill was organizing his terrible autopsy tools into a new leather bag stamped with his initials, *S.A.D.*

"You shouldn't use your middle initial, Sam—I mean, given our profession," she said. He looked at her in a way that said he couldn't imagine why she would say that.

For most of an hour, she suffered his arched eyebrows and head shakes. Yes, she had found the suspect in Maricopa, and she had let her go free on a promise of showing up for the inquest.

"If it had been someone important killed, you know. I'd have to fire you right now," he said. "And if she doesn't show, the sheriff will never let me forget the fact that I hired you, and maybe that's right. Maybe you're not suited to the job."

"If she doesn't show, I'll resign," Antonia said.

"Well, that's something. We'll hope for the best."

The best, in his opinion, is that I fail and go home to San Francisco.

Antonia knew how the grapevine of news and rumor twisted through the faro tables and the bars of

Montezuma Street, and she knew Dill and the sheriff would be feeding it before the day was half over. It would be along the lines of how the whore who killed the other whore was on her way back to town to tell everything, including some political dirt, and would be staying at a hotel too good for her.

During the noon hour, Antonia walked the short way from the plaza up a hill to the Pioneer Home. Great cauliflower towers of clouds fully filled the horizon and framed a blue patch of clear sky above the town.

A stubbed granite promontory to the west called Thumb Butte, visible from anywhere in town, made it easy for any daylight walker to keep their bearings, as it did for still-newcomer Antonia.

The Pioneer Home, funded by the territorial government, had recently celebrated its opening. Its three grand double-deck porches were designed to overlook the town with space for any number of wheelchairs and rocking chairs. Antonia had already made two visits to fetch the bodies of the first old-timers to die in the home.

In those visits, she had met and befriended an elderly man employed to entertain the residents with stories of old Arizona. He had been a gold and silver prospector since before the Civil War and had told Antonia some of his best. He said he never found much metal of value but had made a decent living, because an ambitious prospector would get up to a dozen businessmen in town to stake them for a share of any findings. It was more legal than a lottery, and it had paid off for investors now and then. The trick for a prospector, he told her, was to keep your grubstake subscriptions high and your expenses low.

She found him on a breezy porch and sat down with him.

"Mr. McNary, can I ask you something and ask you not to tell anybody that I asked you?"

"Okay, but if it's about my being a rich prince condemned to look like an old toad until I am kissed by a beautiful woman, I can't talk about it—it makes me croak," Roscoe McNary replied, closing his eyes and puckering his lips.

"It's a serious matter," Antonia replied.

He touched her hand. "Okay, I won't tell a soul, but I probably don't know what you're looking for. I'm mostly bullshit if you'll excuse my French."

"Buffalo Joe—have you heard of him? A local man."

"Well, yes, but you're getting into rough territory. I don't know what you heard, but some things is best left alone. Would you like a coffee, instead? I make good cowboy coffee, the real way. You ever had the real thing?"

"You know what, Mr. McNary? The next time you take the train to Frisco, ask me before you go, and I'll steer you to some Italian places that make coffee almost as good as yours. I love good coffee, but right now I need some help. What can you tell me?"

"Let's take a walk," he said and led her down the front of the hill to a rocky lip where they could sit privately if less comfortably.

"I'll tell you what, miss, one of these days Arizona is going to be a state. We've been a territory long enough. It's going to happen. I think we're just a year or two away."

"That's what I hear, Mr. McNary. Are you changing the subject?"

"I ain't. I wish I was, and I wish you'd call me Roscoe. I shouldn't tell you what I'm going to tell you, but as you're the only one lately who will suffer my stories, I guess I will, as I'd rather be shot than have to shut up.

"Now here's the situation," he began. "Thirteen years or so ago, when we had that dustup with Spain in Cuba, Teddy Roosevelt started asking for cowboys to join a regiment and go down there and kick Spanish backside. Did you know Teddy is coming to these parts in a few days? I just can't imagine it. I'm going to see him, for sure. They say he'll be at the train station and run down to the plaza to see the statue.

"Anyways, I don't know if you know it, but Teddy had a pretty good ranch in the Dakotas. He went out there to cheer himself up after his wife and his mother died. They did that on the same day, if you can believe it, and so he was real down. He finally cheered up enough to go back East, but when the war started with Spain, he remembered that cowboys are tough customers, so he puts out ads recruiting for a regiment of so-called rough riders. I guess you've seen the statue we put up to the ones who didn't make it back. Do you know why those fellas joined up?"

"Men like to soldier off to war," she answered.

"Well, maybe some do. But not these. I mean, very young men do that, mostly for the uniform to impress the ladies. But this war wasn't like that. You had fellows like Buckey O'Neill pushing for men to join up. He was Prescott's damn mayor, not some kid, 'scuse my French, and had been sheriff and county treasurer and other stuff and was an investor in the St. Mick and in mines here and about, including up at the Grand Canyon. He did more than talk: he signed himself up and got two hundred others to follow him. They weren't after the uniforms, and they didn't give a hoot about what the Spaniards were up to in Cuba, but if you want to know who the Rough Riders were, they were Prescott fellers following Buckey. He was our Teddy. Everybody loved that fellow. When he won an election one time, folks carried him in a torch parade all the way to his house so his wife would be real proud."

"Why did they go?"

"Well, I'll tell you: statehood for Arizona. They saw glory in this little war as their ticket. In fact, just as they were leaving Arizona for Cuba, they had a big goodbye dinner at the Ford down in Phoenix, and Buckey makes this toast, he says, 'to victory and a star—who wouldn't die for another star?'—meaning a star on the U.S. flag. Well, he got himself shot dead right through the mouth in Cuba, and we lost a bunch of good men down there—and still no statehood. Congress still turned us down. All we got to show for it was that statue, which we paid for ourselves, and is kind of stupid, as the boat that took the Rough Riders to Cuba didn't have room for their horses like the statue shows. Only Teddy had a horse. Our fellows died to make him famous. Anyway, I think some fellers believed that the spirits of those dead were not going to rest until we got our due, and that would be statehood."

Antonia and Roscoe McNary were sitting on a wide rock overlooking the town.

"Okay, I'm going to keep talking. But you never heard me say any of this next thing. Do you understand?"

"Yes, sir."

"So, after the war, Roosevelt becomes governor of New York and is pushing for all sorts of reforms to favor regular people over the big companies. The big hats figure they can shut him up by sticking him in the vice presidency under McKinley, which office is a known box canyon of sorts. So, that's what they do.

"Now, miss, some of the men in town here, and their daddies, have done rough things. They've wiped out Indian villages, men, women, and children. They've hung cattle thieves and train robbers and men they figured looked guilty enough. It was a tough part of the world and still is, and folks get used to thinking that killing is a part of progress. You ever heard of a man named King Woolsey? I knew him."

"No. I haven't heard the name."

"I think of him when I think of those days," McNary said. "The U.S. Army was around here to protect all the gold and silver mining that was going on, but the Civil War got the Army otherwise engaged, and some of the Apache started up with the killing again—it's their land, of course. So, King Woolsey and some others, but mostly him and fellows he recruited, made a project of killing as many as they could.

"He set up a peace conference with Apache leaders over near Globe. When the Apache showed up, interested in the proposition, Woolsey's men just killed them all. Then another time, he called a peace meeting for the Yavapai around here, and they weren't ever much trouble. But he got them to come, and he knew their families would travel with them because they just do. He knew they would be hungry, as it was winter. Anyway, he put out a big bag of baking flour, because he knew the families would find it and eat it, and they did, and it was poisoned with strychnine and everybody died—every man, woman, and child. So, these were men who didn't mind taking the lives of human beings if they were in their way. And then they went to church on Sunday."

"Was he ever arrested for any of that?"

"Arrested? The Territorial Legislature gave him a damn medal and appointed him head of a state militia. This is who we're talking about, and their sons and grandsons are tough that way, too. They are not the kind to let a fat politician like McKinley stand between them and statehood when their man Roosevelt could be in the White House instead. You see where I'm going?"

"I do," she said.

"So, Woolsey is long dead by 1901, but his spirit was still strutting the earth and was no doubt hovering in a room at the St. Mike when a small group of big hats had a meeting one night and somebody said it was a crying shame that Teddy wasn't the president, because he was just the man who could deliver us our statehood, and, by the way, he could sign the law we were trying to get through Congress to build us a big dam to give us reliable water, the lack of which was another impediment to statehood. Teddy owed us that, as we gave him more than half his Rough Riders, and many of those fellers including Buckey got killed for him. And then someone said it would be a real shame if President McKinley had an accident or got himself killed by some crazy man. And someone said that was enough talk and nobody should say another word, but that's all it took.

"And let me be clear, these men were not Rough Riders themselves; they was just big hats and the kind of men who got others to go off and get themselves killed in Cuba. Anyway, they put together a little pot of money to send Joe Willis to go find some crazy anarchist back East and set him up to shoot McKinley, and that's what happened. It happened in Buffalo, and that's why they call Joe by that nickname. He is still around and is not someone you would ever want to have dealings with. He buys and sells ranches and mines and is mean as sin."

"How do you know all this, Roscoe?"

"Not from rumors. When at my best, I had maybe twenty fellows who staked me in my prospecting. I was privy to a lot of conversations as I sat waiting around for fellers to fetch a bank draw for me. Anyways, it's common knowledge. Of course, Teddy came and went through the presidency, and he ain't president anymore, but while he was, these fellows got him to sign the law that built a big dam for Arizona and will likely turn parts of the state into one of the breadbaskets of the nation. So that was a pretty good bit of progress, and most say we'll be a state in just a year or three—soon as that water starts flowing full time.

"Old Teddy is coming here in a few days to dedicate the new dam, you know. Did I already say that? They named it after him—the big dam. World's largest by ten times, they say. He ain't president anymore, because he counted McKinley's term that he took over as his own first term, and so only ran once after that, leaving the nomination to Taft. He could have run again, but he thought that was the square thing to do. Then Taft starts cutting all Teddy's prize reforms out of the herd, and so now Teddy is thinking of challenging him for the nomination. Taft himself was in town a bit over a year ago, probably trying to undercut Teddy's chances. He stayed right down there and had curious meetings at the St. Mick."

With that, Roscoe McNary pointed down the hill at what he thought was the Hotel St. Michael. He was off by enough that Antonia could see he was nearly blind.

"Teddy is for the people, you know, and for Arizona, so that's who the Republicans should nominate next year. But that's all done in cigar smoke, so don't place your bet just yet. And some of these hats don't believe much in elections, anyway.

"I'll shut up now about all this and about you asking about it, but you had better pretend you didn't hear any of it."

"I will," Antonia said. "And let's see if this works…" With that, she leaned over and kissed him on the cheek.

He looked at his still-grizzled hands.

"Didn't work. Maybe a hug?" he asked.

Near Iron Springs

4. Sunset Ledge

Antonia reserved a room at the St. Michael in Elsie's name and walked down to Sheldon Street where she rented a horse and surrey to fetch Elsie from Iron Springs. She was there in two hours.

"There'll be enough activity on Montezuma so people will see us arriving at the hotel," she told Elsie inside Mike Wall's rough cabin. "I've already told Dill that I am heading out of town for a day on personal business, leaving you in the hotel alone. I promised I'd be back in time for the inquest, which is the day after tomorrow. But I won't leave town; I'll go in the back way of the hotel and be there with you every minute."

"Will we have room service? How will we eat."

"Yes, I suppose we will."

"They're going to think I'm a pig, as I'll be ordering for two."

Elsie then got a strange look and stood very still.

"Do you smell that?" Elsie whispered.

"What?"

"Cowboy," she said, still in a whisper. "Which way is the breeze going tonight?" Elsie crouched down a bit, spread out her arms and hands, and turned in several directions, her nose sniffing the air. "I can't tell where it's coming from," she whispered.

Antonia almost laughed but then took it seriously. "It's very still tonight," she whispered, pulling her pistol from her handbag. She moved quietly to the door and snugged a board onto iron clips on the jambs to bar it from the inside. The windows were closed for the season by shutters that locked from the outside. The back door was barred.

"You really think you can smell someone out there? You can really do that?" she whispered.

"Just got a little whiff, but yes," Elsie replied. "Maybe there's just a pile of dirty laundry in here somewhere, but I guess I would have smelled it before. I think someone is outside."

"Anyway," Antonia said in full voice and with a wink, "You'll be safe here tonight. Let's have a drink and I'll head back to town. I just wanted to make sure you were all right. I'll come fetch you tomorrow afternoon."

Elsie nodded that she understood what was going on, but she grabbed Antonia's arm and whispered, "Listen, miss, don't leave me."

Antonia put her lips to Elsie's ear.

"Elsie, if there is someone out there—smart or stupid—maybe someone who followed me from town or got word from the conductor that you were here— then they're going to wait for me to leave here before they make a move on you. They know that shooting a saloon girl and maybe making it look like you shot yourself, is going to go down easier than if a deputy coroner gets killed. So, they will wait for me to leave. All you need to do is keep the door barred and stay calm as a cucumber long enough for me to tie up my rig a little up the road and come back through the woods and wait for the move to happen. This isn't the way I wanted to do this, but we can turn it around on them. Will you do this?"

Elsie nodded. "I don't suppose you have another pistol in your bag, do you? The windows aren't barred."

"Sorry, I don't. But this wouldn't be much of a cabin if there weren't a shotgun or a .22 in here. Have you looked around?" Antonia asked.

"I looked last night. Nothing. The only thing I saw was a kid's slingshot."

"Okay. Well, go get that. And there's a Chinese Checkers game over there. Get a marble or two. If you can put someone's eye out, that gives you a few seconds to run like hell. But I'll get him first. Bolt the door when I go out, then get somewhere in a corner, down on the floor, in case some shots come through the place."

Antonia drove the little rig away from the cabin and up the road, where she tied the horse to a branch near the community's main gate and patted the horse's head and told it to keep quiet. She then began moving as fast as the dark would allow through alligator pines and sharp manzanita. The closer she came to the cabin the more careful she was to not step on anything that would snap.

She heard the evening train coming through. It wasn't slowing, as it only stopped when there was a passenger coming or going, and that was rare except in summer. But the noise gave her cover to move quickly and quietly. When silence returned, she was whispering distance to a corner of the cabin. She could see no one. The quarter moon was low but just enough that, if someone were there, she should see him.

"I'll have that pistol, miss," a voice came from just behind her. She could smell him now. She raised her hands, and he pulled the gun from her fingers.

She figured he couldn't be Buffalo Joe Willis himself, given the smell. Willis was a rich man, at least compared to most in the area. This was a hired man, a trigger man—the knife man. But she figured Buffalo Joe had sent him, and so she took a chance on that.

"I don't know who you are," she said, "but Joe is going to be plenty mad if you get in my way tonight."

"Joe who?" he said.

"Joe Willis. He hired me to make sure the whore don't get to town any time soon, or ever," she said.

"He did not, miss. I followed you tonight from town. I know very well who you are, miss."

"Maybe you think you know what's going on," Antonia said, "but Joe isn't simple in his plans, is he? I hate that he calculated he needed you and me and the sheriff to make sure it got done."

She could feel his confusion. She turned around to face him, her hands still up. He looked very rough—dirty even by moonlight. His beard was half-gray and a year too long. He was big, at least three inches above six feet. She knew she was looking at the killer of Agnes Bailey. He was wearing a filthy fringed jacket that made him look like a mangy wolf on its hind legs.

"You smell like a skunk," she said.

He laughed. "The gals say that. But they get used to it when they have to."

"You can count me out."

"We'll see about that," he snorted and made a rotten-tooth smile that showed against the grime of his beard. He leveled his pistol at her chest.

"I got an idea," he said, "I think I'll tell ol' Joe that the whore shot you dead, and it were just lucky I was there to get the whore. But maybe you and I can have a little fun first

His smile got bigger, and his eyes were bulging with fun. She was building up to kick him in his groin and hope for the best, but just then a glass marble hit the center of his forehead full force and stuck there for a moment. He stood stunned long enough for Antonia to kick him like she planned and then kick the guns from his hands. Both pistols went flying into the dark brush. Her foot suddenly hurt terribly from the blue steel. She found her gun where she thought it had fallen and then spun around to point it at him or shoot, but he had started running away through the brush. She followed.

"Don't shoot me, lady!" he yelled as he ran.

"You stop or I'll shoot you down," she yelled back.

He reached an outcropping of granite boulders and scrambled up in the darkness. She followed. He found himself on a narrow crack of a ledge, high above a rocky landing below. The adventurous summer children of Iron Springs called it Sunset Ledge.

"Looky here, lady! I got myself into a fix here. I were just kidding. If Joe sent you, then we're partners in this. We need to get back there to that cabin and take care of our dark business."

"I don't know, friend," she replied. "We might not have the kind of trust between us for any of that. Why don't you just tell me where I can find Joe and settle this?"

She then growled and cocked the gun again in case he didn't hear it the first time.

"I guess I'll just have to shoot you," she said.

"No ma'am don't do it, pretty please. I got big plans this Saturday and I'd hate to miss 'em. And Joe ain't in town. He ain't even in Arizony."

"So, where is he? Where was he when he told you to do this? Oh, you're not going to tell me, are you? You're going to die tonight, and Joe won't care a whit, will he?" Antonia growled and cocked the gun again.

The man was clearly not comfortable with heights. He glanced downward as her predatory tone and her cocking and re-cocking of her gun made him inch ever farther along the narrowing ledge. His boots were too big for it and were rocking nervously on the crumbly two-inch crack.

"I sent him a wire and told him I mighta got drunk and talked too much the other night. He said to just take care of it, which I did, to the cost of my soul, I guess, and like I'm tryin' to do tonight with the talkety one. Joe let me buy a gun on his account this morning.—I ain't afforded one in a while. He sent me a tellygram today to tell me to follow you and tonight and get the girl tomorrow at the St. Mick, if she weren't with you tonight. I'm just following orders, cleaning up my own mess. You can't blame me for that, particularly if we're on the same side, here."

"If you have that telegram on you, I'll trade it for your life," Antonia said. "I'm the law here, more or less, but I got no way to get you into town and I'm not going to shoot you unarmed if I don't have to, so give it to me and I'll back away and find you some other day. You'll get a head start."

"Well, that's mighty square. Let me see if I got it here in my pocket."

"If you pull a little gun on me, or even if I half-think you are, I'll shoot. I can see better in the dark than you, old man."

"Yes, ma'am. I ain't got no more guns. I got the tellygram here."

He pulled a wadded paper from his shirt pocket. It seemed to be the yellow of a telegram, though it was hard for Antonia to be sure in the near dark.

"Reach it out to me slowly," she said.

"All right now. Here comes." He stretched his right arm toward her, pressing his back hard against the granite. She kept the gun pointed at his face with her right hand and reached her left toward him.

Their hands were an inch apart when he lunged for her wrist. She pulled away fast enough to save herself, but his move sent him off balance. The telegram fluttered down as he watched it and then felt himself going.

"Damn, damn!" he said as he tumbled down against the granite slope. His skull cracked on a flat stone far below and, even by moonlight, she could see the blood flooding out from his ruined head.

She climbed down to confirm the death and to retrieve the telegram. She went through his pockets but found only a cheap watch, a half-gone plug of tobacco, and about twenty dollars in coin. She relieved him of his gun belt, as it had ammunition on it, and her coroner's training would not allow her to leave it there. She found a receipt wadded in the tip of the holster. There was just enough light to make it out: He had purchased the gun at Sam Hill Hardware the day before but had put it on the account of Joe Willis. It showed his own name as Andrew Wolf—a good name for him, she thought. She looked again at his watch, still working, to note the time of death.

The telegram was brief: "JUST FOLLOW HER SHE WILL LEAD YOU TO MISS BRAIDS."

The sender was "WILLIS ST FRANCIS HOTEL SAN FRAN."

You're no mastermind, Buffalo Joe, to put such evidence in writing. Did you think he was smart enough to burn it? Or the receipt from the gun?

Antonia knew the St. Francis well. It was one of the showplaces gutted by fire in the earthquake that had recently reopened.

She pulled a few of the longer hairs from his beard and wrapped them in the gun receipt. She then took off his jacket and put it over his face. She made a prayer and apologized to God for taking a life, though he fell on his own account.

On her way back through the dark to the cabin, she called out several times that it was just her coming and that everything was now safe, as she didn't want to lose an eye to a marble. She remembered her foot and began to favor it with a limp.

"If he has a gun on you, be brave and say so," Elsie said from inside.

"He does not; he is dead, my friend."

Elsie, who had learned some nursing on the job, wrapped the ankle in a pillowcase torn to strips and gave Antonia a shoulder as they made their way through the dark to the surrey.

"How come you don't got a man?" Elsie asked as they stepped high through fallen branches.

"Where's your manners—to ask me such a personal thing!"

"I don't need manners so much. Why did Mike let you know where the key is hid? Have you been here with him? He must have at least brought you here to show you the right cabin and how to get in?"

"He was showing me around town and hereabouts when I was new in Prescott," Antonia replied. "Don't make anything of it, please."

"Fine, but it's quite aways out of town. Don't tell me a thing. None of my business."

"Have you ever been to San Francisco?" Antonia asked.

"I have not," Elsie answered. "And I might think you are just changing the subject, but I have the feeling you are trying to get me on the hook again."

"I surely am," Antonia replied. "I can get this Joe Willis arrested in San Francisco. I can do that based on my own testimony and this telegram and gun receipt. He sent it from San Francisco, so his part of the crime is there. I bet he has no political pull in San Francisco to get himself off, like he probably does in Prescott. And you coming with me is a good idea just because I don't know if you're safe in Prescott, and San Francisco is probably where you want to go anyway."

"I never have seen an opera—not a real one, with the costumes not coming off the ladies. Not a pretty one. Maybe we could go to one?" Elsie asked.

"That's fine. We'll see one if we can."

Antonia let the surrey horse find their way back to Prescott, as starlight and a moon were stuck in the forest branches and barely showed the road.

"You seem shaken," Elsie said. "You ever been in a close scrape like that before?"

"I don't know. Maybe," Antonia said.

"Just before he fell he was sort of frozen in the moment, you know? Suspended in the air, like. And I was thinking, just in that half a second, maybe I could grab him and save him. But I figured there was a good chance that would send me over, too. And I was calculating that, maybe if I saved him, he would want to kill me anyway. But that pitiable look on his face in that moment—I can't get it out."

"I woulda just gave him a little kick," Elsie replied. "You and me is different."

"You and I *are* different."

"And if I didn't get him with that slingshot, we'd both be dead right now. I don't know why you figured it would be safer for me out here in a cabin. I would'a been safer in town. How'd he know where I was, anyway? I'm so happy that my life is in your care."

"He followed me out from town. He told me that. I should have been more careful."

They separately and silently turned over the facts as they rode.

"I should'a stole Mike's slingshot," was one of Elsie's few out-loud thoughts. "I did as good with it as you did with your gun—better, if you think about it."

Mostly to change the subject, Antonia asked Elsie how she had met Agnes Bailey.

"We were kinda on the auction block together," Elsie said, and told her story in bits as they traveled the dark miles into town.

She had been one of the last of the young people from an orphan train out of Boston to be taken in by a Kansas City family. She figured the reluctance to pick her was all about her skin tone, as she could see the frowns whenever a visiting husband and wife walked through the wards and lawns of the settlement house, mostly looking for another child to work their farm.

The one husband who did pick her said yes, "if she's all you got."

The man's wife didn't seem to have any say. She wouldn't even look Elspeth Corcoran in the eye—that was her birth name and her name at the Boston Home for Little Wanderers, but it was no longer the name she called herself.

"I was Elsie Cork before I left Boston," she said.

The man's wife did talk to her later that first day, in the tiny room that would be her own. The conversation was brief and one-sided. Elsie was informed that several other girls had been adopted but had run away.

"I hope you, Elspeth, run away, too," the wife said. "And if you decide to, you'll find a sack in your closet with some clothes your size and a bit of money. It will be there as of tomorrow, and there's always bread in the breadbox."

Elsie took that as most unwelcoming, but it was the right thing for the woman to offer, as Elsie would learn on the third night. She resisted the husband's advances with the help of a broken water glass and was gone that same night.

She knew the name of the family that had taken in her best friend, Agnes. She found the farm and was planning to live secretly in their barn, but Agnes also had a hard story to tell. It had more to do with backbreaking work and beatings by the wife than anything to do with the husband.

It took only two midnight conversations for Agnes to agree to run away with Elsie to Abilene, Kansas— Elsie had heard the town was nice.

They found work there in laundries and café kitchens. Agnes met a young man who asked her to marry him and move to Buffalo where his uncle had a lumber mill and a job for him. She accepted, soon to her regret, as the young man drank too much and thought beating a wife was as good a way as any to unwind after a day of being yelled at by a boss who wanted to fire him but couldn't.

Elsie and Agnes stayed in touch by writing, as Elsie stayed on in Abilene and was soon working downstairs in a bar and then upstairs, where she stayed for several years before meeting a young man from Arizona.

Willie Thayne was from a ranching family that owned an entire valley near Prescott. He had been to Abilene several years in a row with his father to negotiate the annual sale of their Arizona cattle but had come this time on his own, as his father was in a sickbed and would die within months.

Elsie was Willie's first. Willie was Elsie's first, but in other ways. He was the first man she felt something like love for, and the first she had told her story to.

He had a shock of red hair that exploded out from around his cowboy hat like a housefire and a face so smooth and full of big features that she sometimes laughed just to look at him, which made him laugh back. He always had a big smile anyway.

"Well, we gotta get you out'a this place, Elsie," is what he said that made her throw away most of her clothes, buy some fresh, and say goodbye to the owner of the bar, the madame atop the stairs, and the few rough friends she had made among the women. She was taking the train to Arizona with rich boy Willie Thayne, and against the madame's warnings that he would not feel the same way about her, once he got back around his family and they asked him if he was crazy.

Elsie suggested to Willie that he say she was a teacher in Abilene. "Well, you done taught me a few things!" he said in agreement.

"And say I'm Black Irish," she asked.

The teacher part worked with Willie's mother, but she knew what Black Irish was and wasn't, and knew that Elsie wasn't. That made the mother pry into the teaching part and an atmosphere of cold suspicion thickened between them.

Willie and Elsie's marriage plans kept getting delayed by the inventions of the mother, including her own health complaints, which were clearly improvised.

Willie submitted to his mother's idea that Elsie should have an apartment in Prescott, which was nearly an hour's ride. Willie came to her more often than she was invited to the ranch, and she could see Willie's smile become thinner and rarer until it was mostly not there at all.

He was running his horse one morning when a hoof broke through a prairie dog tunnel and broke the leg and sent Willie tumbling down a rocky slope. He didn't make it.

His mother, after his burial, told Elsie that it was crazy for him to be riding hard in a place like that, known to be full of prairie dog holes. She was hinting that Elsie had driven him crazy and so he wasn't acting with any sense. Elsie told her in a quiet voice that if anybody drove him crazy, it was her, and that he really did love her, and they would have had a wonderful family and wonderful life and given her beautiful grandchildren.

Elsie stayed in town and started working in the restaurant at the St. Michael and then in the bars.

After one last letter from Agnes in Buffalo, telling of a brutal beating, Elsie sent Agnes the money for a train ticket to Prescott, Arizona.

"That's who killed her—me," Elsie said to Antonia, just as they pulled close to the livery barn in Prescott. From there, they walked and limped up to Antonia's room in a rooming house.

At dawn, Antonia decided her ankle was fine and resolved not to limp. She woke Elsie and they dressed for a long day and for travel. First was a bite of breakfast downstairs and then a buggy ride up to the Pioneer Home, as Antonia didn't want to leave Elsie alone in the rooming house and didn't trust the courthouse.

At the Pioneer Home, Antonia asked Roscoe McNary to take care of Elsie for a few hours by telling her stories from his past.

In the Coroner's Office, Antonia explained to Chief Coroner Dill that there was a body waiting to be fetched from Iron Springs, drawing a map to show where to find it. She explained further that Elsie could not be a suspect in her roommate's murder, and she laid out the reasons. She asked for the inquest to be delayed until further notice, as her own testimony would be expected, and she thought she needed to go immediately to San Francisco to see about the arrest of "Buffalo Joe" Willis.

Dill just stared at her as she finished. She couldn't tell if he was angry or impressed.

"You'll be outside your jurisdiction. You'll need some more money," he finally said, finding the petty cash box. "You want me to have the sheriff lock her up for her own safety while you're gone?"

"No, sir. I'm taking her with me," she replied. "I don't think she's safe in this town, even in jail. Please don't tell a soul, even the sheriff, that I'm taking her with me."

He nodded in a way that made her certain he knew things she didn't, but that he would respect her confidence—for her safety if not for Elsie's.

"Give my compliments to your father when you get to Frisco," he said. She nodded

Percival Lowell

5. Meeting Percy

The short train ride north to Ash Fork was without conversation. There, Antonia and Elsie boarded the mainline railroad west to Needles and then on through the desert and northward beside the Pacific Range to San Francisco.

Owing to Dill's ungenerous advance, they sat in regular coach seats but had no trouble sleeping in plush chairs facing each other.

At about 2 a.m. they were awakened by a man who stood in the aisle and was intent on talking. Though the lighting was dim, the shine of his bald head was visible, as were wild whisps of white hair from his temples and from his joyful mustache.

"Ladies, you seem to be alone in this car, and this will be a long night. Have you forgotten to go to your compartment?"

"We will sleep here. Thank you, we are fine," Antonia said.

He sat down next to Elsie in order to engage Antonia. At the same time, he caught the eye of a night porter and put a finger up to call him over. He ordered himself a brandy and offered service to the ladies. They declined.

"It helps me sleep," he said. "I should put my feet near the window in my compartment, but I always put my head there so I can look up and see the night sky, and that gets me thinking about the planets and stars, and the next thing I know, it's dawn. So, the brandy is healthy if it helps me get some rest. If I may introduce myself, I am Percival Lowell, a resident of Flagstaff but originally of Massachusetts."

He extended his hand to both women, who shook it because he was clearly a gentleman. They introduced themselves.

"We are traveling together to the Coast," Antonia offered.

Lowell pulled a small leatherbound notebook and a gold mechanical pencil from his inside pocket and wrote a few things down in the dim light.

"What are you writing?" Elsie asked sleepily.

"Your names, in the event we meet again. At my age, I make this accommodation."

"Are you describing us?" she continued, "you seem to be writing quite a lot."

"I am describing you, yes: you by very large brown eyes and by your lovely braids, Miss Cork, which you must never alter, if only for the accuracy of my little notebook."

"And Miss Bonaventura?" Elsie asked. "How do you describe her?"

"Her great curly hair of course. It is joyful to look at. And her plumpish lips, if she is not pouting and if she will not mind my saying so. I think her eyes may be green, though it is hard to tell in here. I will add the question mark. I will further note with the initials KM that she reminds me of Kathleen, the girl in third grade who got away. And I will ask you, Miss Bonaventura, not to refer to me, as did she, as Nursey Percy—a cruelty occasioned by the fact that I was not permitted to walk to school alone, but with a governess who wore a white uniform and came again to walk me home."

"Oh, my!" Elsie said, "You really grew up rich, didn't you? And Nursey Percy? You mustn't give away such ammunition. Women, I'm sure you know, are heartless and cannot have such a delicious thing without using it when it comes to having an argument with you, which will happen sooner or later. Where does all that money come from, if I may ask?"

By reflex, Antonia started to give Elsie's ankle a little kick but realized it would be seen and so aborted it. It was seen, anyway.

"Miss Antonia, you were about to kick your friend," Lowell said. "Please be my guest."

The little shared laugh warmed the conversation, and Lowell answered the question.

"Cotton and woolen mills, Miss Cork," Lowell said. "Nearly every garment in your wardrobe comes from mills that send me a penny or two. It adds up."

With his brandy in hand, Lowell smiled at her without having something else particular to say and then gestured to the window:

"The stars out here in the desert are remarkable. I don't know if you have noticed—or can notice through the grime on this glass—but the clear desert air is marvelous. The stars and planets are my special interest, and I have a rather fine refracting telescope on a hill above Flagstaff for their examination—a twenty-four-incher."

He held his hands wide with his jiggling brandy at one end to indicate the size of the lens.

"You are the Mars fellow," Elsie offered.

"I am. I have made a study of it."

"If you are looking for volunteers, I should like to go to Mars," she replied.

"Miss, I shall place you second in line, right after myself."

"And I gather from your books that you rather think there is a race of men up there, making canals and all," Elsie continued.

Antonia, but half-awake, was impressed that Elsie was carrying the conversation so well.

"A race of men. Well, I expect we can—the three of us—agree that there are already enough men in the Universe. Let us hope they are a race of gentlewomen," Lowell said to Elsie.

"Are you a teacher, Miss Cork? How do you come by my books?"

"Alas, no, Mr. Lowell, I am a common prostitute," she said, just to see if he would be shocked. "But I make a point of spending time with books when time permits, and I have had clients who are teachers and professors and, because they are usually poorly paid, I have given extra time and joy in exchange for the borrowing of books. Yours are quite popular, as I'm sure you must know. For a time, I had your book on the *Occult Practices of Japan*, which I found fascinating, though I was hoping for a more sensual read than it provided."

"Common, my foot. You are not common in the least," he said, slapping his own knee and catching his brandy from a near spill. "By the way, I have several copies in my bag of my newest book, though it is again about Mars and again has nothing of the erotic. I will give you one. But this sleeping in the coach car.... now look," he said, summoning the porter to return, "you have got my thinking all excited and I'm not going to get a wink of sleep anyway, so my compartment will go to waste."

"Eddie," Lowell said to the porter, handing him a coin that looked substantial, "pack away my things enough so that these ladies can have my room for the night, will you? And, ladies, I will hold your seats here, and I will see you for breakfast. Eddie, pull one of the books out of my initialed bag and leave it out for this lady. And miss, you must bring it along to breakfast and I will make a nice inscription in it for you."

Antonia resisted the gift of the room, but Lowell would not be denied his largess. The porter said there would be no difficulty, and he grabbed the women's bags from the overhead and led them to the largest of the train's compartments.

The room was ornate in its dark woods, brass appointments, and elegant upholstery fabrics and bedding. The porter, after fetching from Lowell's bag a copy of *The Evolution of Worlds* for Elsie, turned down an upper bed so that both women could sleep in luxury until the sun woke them in the bumps and lurches of the Sierra foothills.

Traveling from the wilds of the Arizona Territory to civilized San Francisco in little more than twenty-four hours was the regular experience for younger people like Antonia and Elsie, but for the older Mr. Lowell, it was still something of a modern miracle.

"I can't get over it," he said at breakfast, after signing his book for Elsie. "I'm sure you've heard people of my age—I'm nearly 60, if you can believe it—talk about how long it used to take by stage, and even longer by wagon. You said, Miss Cork, that you would like to take a trip to Mars. Well, how far off can that be, the way things are changing, one invention after another, almost every day? And my field, astronomy, is not to be left behind—huge telescopes are in the works."

His wispy white temples seemed to sparkle with electricity and his face reddened as he inhaled the imagining of it.

The ambiance of the dining car was enhanced by Lowell's familiarity with the porters, who brought champagne and sweet rolls at his command. By the time the eggs, bacon, biscuits, and gravy arrived, Antonia and Elsie could only pick at their plates.

"Do you realize," Lowell went on, holding a small potato up on the tines of his fork, "how much there is yet to see out there? The stars you see when you look up at night—any clear night—are hardly the whole story. Our planet and our sun are small potatoes in a large swirl of stars and planets. This might make you feel very small, but I think you can just see it as the grandeur of creation, and we should celebrate it. I'm not very religious, but my, it's quite a creation and a good excuse for religion if you need one."

He fingered a cigar and smelled it but resisted lighting it. He tucked it back into the handkerchief pocket of his suit jacket. His outfit was finely tailored but his scuffed cowboy boots were an odd match for it. He crossed a leg under the dining table in a way that made difficulties for passers-by.

"And some astronomers here and there—am I boring you? I am certainly boring you, but this will be the last of it: Some of the stars you see are not stars at all, but other giant swirls of stars, just like our swirl."

"Galaxies," Elsie offered.

"Exactly so. Brava," Lowell replied. "And that's enough about my interests. Let's hear about yours. What occasions a businesswoman and her friend to travel to the land of the Golden Gate? I will say you are both interesting enough that it might well be a lecture tour."

"It is not," Antonia said. In speaking those few words, she realized the champagne was hitting hard. She was afraid of sounding tipsy or of sharing too much information, but she had trust in this near stranger, as champagne will do.

"We are in pursuit of a killer by the name of Joseph Willis—so called Buffalo Joe. We think he may be in San Francisco—in the St. Francis, to be exact. One of his henchmen tried to kill Elsie last evening near Prescott and did kill her friend the morning of the day before. I more or less killed that fellow last evening, though Elsie was a big help. This Buffalo Joe is behind these attacks, and I have had too much champagne."

Lowell processed the information for a moment, his head nodding everything into place.

"Ah, my condolence, Miss Cork. My deep condolence for the loss of your friend. And my condolence to her spirit, for it is such a terribly immense thing to lose life itself and all the joys and beauty that it might yet have brought her. And I am glad you were not among this villain's victims."

Elsie lowered her head and was clearly moved. Lowell put his hand on her shoulder and said that he wasn't much for prayer but that he did so from time to time, out of an abundance of caution. He lowered his head in silence for ten or so seconds.

"Let's talk about San Francisco," he then said. "I'm staying—I always stay—at the Palace Hotel on Market Street—the new Palace, of course, since we lost the old one in '06. I used to stay at the Mark Hopkins, and I hear it may come back soon. Anyway, I shall move my quarters upon our arrival to the St. Francis and I will be of whatever service you ask of me. I have great resources, and not from my telescope work, which only drains my accounts. Speaking of money, I have seen your travel budget, if one may judge by your ticket class on the train, so I should like to see that you have a room there, too, and on the ladies' floor, of course."

"It would be most convenient," Antonia said, "but I have family in the city, but thank you, anyway."

"Well, Miss Bonaventura, I have gained from my telescope work the conclusion that one learns best when one looks closest, so I think you will be more successful if you allow me to participate in this way, putting you right in the thick of things. I am a benefactor for many good causes, and criminal justice may as well be among them."

Antonia knew that her budget would soon be exhausted in expensive San Francisco, and she would be personally financing their expenses.

Would he have made the offer to two men? No.

"Very well, and thank you, I'm sure you are right," Antonia said. "It will be an advantage for us to be in the hotel where our investigation may be centered."

"And why, Dr. Lowell, are *you* traveling to the city?" Elsie Cork asked. "I do mean Dr. Lowell."

"Oh, I come several times a year, just to renew my artistic sensibilities. Doctor, yes, but the academic sort, so don't call me by it. I am meeting a friend who is returning from the South Pacific after observing an important solar eclipse in Tonga. A long sail, as you can imagine. My observatory loaned him a camera for the event, and he will deliver it into my hands at the dock there. It is not the sort of thing that you put in the care of shipping clerks and stevedores—rather more like a baby, and one of my dearest. I will also see some of the new art that is coming over from France and an opera or two. And some fine dining."

"Operas?" Elsie said.

"Indeed, operas," Lowell repeated after her.

"How very nice that must be," Elsie said, smiling professionally.

6. In a New San Francisco

Lowell hailed a carriage to take them the few blocks to the St. Francis. As they were signing the register, Lowell got to business with the clerk:

"I'm expecting to meet Joseph Willis here in the hotel. Is he registered?"

Antonia was put off balance by his direct action. "Maybe we should settle into our rooms first," she interrupted.

"Quite right," Lowell said to the clerk. "We won't disturb him. Let's just see if he's registered."

"No sir. He was here for several days. He left the morning before last."

"Ah, I was afraid we might be too late. We were delayed. Can you see if arrangements were made for his travel? I'd like to send him a wire to apologize."

"I will have to ask the other clerks and the bell captain. Let me get you into your rooms and I will send you word. Are the ladies to be in an adjoining room to yours, Mr. Lowell?"

"Dr. Lowell, and no, we have presumed they will be roomed on the ladies' floor."

"Since '06, we have not had the luxury of a ladies' floor. But I assure you the hotel is safe. We have two detectives on duty, day and night, and all the doors are double locking."

"That is fine," Lowell said, seeing Antonia and Elsie nodding in agreement. "But not adjoining rooms with me, if you please."

"Of course, sir, I only assumed you were family."

"We are here on business," Lowell replied. "But we shall need three tickets for whichever best opera is playing tonight."

Elsie stood in the middle of their hotel room for a full minute, turning around.

"It's awfully nice," she said, "but why is there no bowl and pitcher? How are we princesses supposed to freshen up?"

"Take a look in that closet," Antonia replied.

"Oh, my god," Elsie said. "We have our own bathtub and toilet and everything!"

After unpacking her small bag, Antonia wrote a note to her father's sister on Castro Street and went down to the lobby to send it by messenger. In a little more than an hour, two boxes arrived at the hotel, containing two dresses worthy of the opera and a note of welcome from her aunt.

Percival Lowell was otherwise engaged. The bell captain had come to his room with the news that Joe Willis did not make his travel arrangements through the hotel, nor did he mention his next destination.

"However," the bell captain said with unease, "I saw him meeting in a side room of the lobby for some time. One of these men is known to me, if that is of interest to you. I might be able to recollect the fellow's name if I pinch my brain a bit."

"Do come in and pinch away," Lowell said, looking for his wallet on the dresser for a five-dollar bill, which he set on a side table next to the captain.

"Have a seat. My own memory also does better when paid," Lowell said.

The captain, who had limped in as he found a chair, slipped it into his pocket.

"I am not giving you the pinch, Dr. Lowell. I would tell you all I remember without the need of a tip, but I thank you for your generosity. Well, sir, I pride myself on names and faces. It's a good knack if you're in my trade. People do like to be remembered. People like to be important to other people, especially in a fine hotel like this."

"It is a very fine hotel. I expect I will stay here many times in the future." Having said that, Lowell sat in an opposite chair and crossed his arms.

"First," he said, "describe this Joe Willis fellow. What does he look like?"

"He looks like a brute in a tuxedo, if I may say so—if I am not giving offense."

"He is hardly a friend, so you are not offending me, but please be more specific."

"A bit on the portly side, but not grossly fat. Well-fed, you would say. Fifty or so. Prosperous. A bushy mustache, gray and brown, and the same eyebrows. Balding on top. Six feet and an inch or so."

"To be clear," Lowell clarified, "this is the Joe Willis fellow from Arizona. Now, how about the man he was meeting—description-wise, and his name if you have it?"

"I do not have his name exactly, Dr. Lowell. But I will say he is well over six feet—maybe six-two—and unusually slim, almost gaunt. Forty years old or thereabouts. Rather like our late President Lincoln, sans beard. In fact, if you wanted to put him in a theatrical play as Mr. Lincoln, it would be a good fit. A pockmarked sort of face and tight skin, small but bright blue eyes—a dangerous-looking fellow."

"How so?"

"He has the look of a man who has been shot once or twice and not much minded. That is, his eyes fix and dart and stare, while his head never moves—as you might expect of a gunfighter of your generation, if I might say—no offense intended."

"None at all, and that will do fine. Good description. I can see him. Thank you."

"He is clearly a party man," the bell captain added. "I don't mean the drinking kind, but the Republican kind. He was in here often of late. I did not know anything about him until several weeks ago when President Taft was our guest, and this man was clearly involved with Taft's people. I am sure he is the same man who was visiting with your Mr. Joseph Willis. They argued at several points, but they did shake hands as they parted."

"His name?"

"Again sir, I do not have it exactly. He was not here as a guest, or I would have searched the register for him before coming to you. I believe Mr. Willis once called him by a name that I'm not sure of at all."

"And the name?"

"Davis, I believe, but he may have been talking about someone else by that name. I could only catch bits of their conversation, and even that was by accident, as I didn't know it would be important. And one more thing: He smokes a particular cigar. I don't know the brand, but he was upset in front of Mr. Willis that our cigar counterman did not carry it, and we carry nearly all the best from Cuba and so forth."

"Anything else?"

"A well-cut suit. His gait was normal. No cane, either, even for show. I don't like gents who carry canes they don't need, sir. I think they do it so they can't be expected to carry anything or open any door, even for themselves."

"I noticed your own slight limp, Captain. That must make your work difficult."

"Not at all, Dr. Lowell. I am proud of that limp, as it came in service to my country in Cuba, and I do have forty boys here who do all the running around for me with luggage and room service and whatnot. So, I am fine."

"You were a Rough Rider?"

"I was not, Dr. Lowell. I served with the regular Marines, but I hold great admiration for that regiment and their leader—Teddy, of course. And I must say, it was all I could do to not throw a punch when Taft's men were all over our bar and restaurant with their crude opinions against Teddy. I know they are concerned that Teddy might run for the White House again, and spoil the fun Taft is having, undoing all of Teddy's reforms."

"Let me know if you remember anything more about that Davis fellow—the Abe Lincoln—who was talking with Willis, will you?"

"I will, sir, and I hope you enjoy your stay, and I hope I did not offend with my political steam. Your opera tickets will be waiting at my desk. The performance begins at eight, but it's best to get there a half-hour early, as I'm sure you know. The hotel carriage will get you there."

"That's fine. And you do not offend; you illuminate. Please take a message right away to Miss Bonaventura and Miss Cork and ask them to meet me in the restaurant as soon as possible."

Lowell wrote in his small notebook everything the man had said and then buffed his own shoes free of train dust.

While waiting for the women near the lobby entrance to the restaurant, he asked the cigar man if he remembered a fellow who was upset about the hotel not having good enough cigars for sale. He did, describing him similarly. He knew the brand of cigar: The Nacional Hotel Grande.

"We haven't carried them since the Spanish War. People objected. It is a political cigar, if I may say so, and a hotel can't afford to offend its guests."

The man knew of one place in town likely to carry them: a large tobacconist across the street from the Republican Party headquarters and downstairs from the Elks Club.

"I shall pay a visit," Lowell said, tipping the man.

"While you are here, would you like a cigar, sir?"

"Thank you, but I am cutting back. In my line, which is star gazing, any smoke can put a haze on the lenses. We are examining things so distant that you cannot even imagine. One particle of smoke might obscure an entire world out there, and possibly a world better than our own."

"May you find one, sir."

7. On the Trail of Slight Clues

"What magic is this?" Lowell said in the lobby as he looked at the two women in the borrowed dresses. Elsie's long braids were curled up around the top of her head, revealing gold loop earrings and a beauty that her braids had not done justice.

"Both dresses are borrowed. Do you think they are suitable for the opera? I had my aunt send them over. My family lives in town," Antonia explained.

"Belles of the ball you shall be. You are both perfect for the opera. But I wanted you to come down so we might have a bite and I'll tell you what I just learned."

They were seated near a window looking onto Geary Street and were served water and menus. The cable cars passing down Powell Street were close enough to see down the way and excited Elsie, who stood up each time she heard their dinging bells to get a better view.

"Your Buffalo Joe Willis was here, and I have a good description of him written down—a fiftyish brute, six or six-one, bushy bearded, balding. He met in the lobby with a political fellow of about forty who is with the Taft campaign or perhaps just with the Republican Party. This second man, whose name may be Davis, has the appearance of Abe Lincoln, tall, very slim, but bare-chinned. The bell captain didn't much like him or the other Taft fellows who were all over the hotel several weeks ago, as was Taft himself. He didn't like them because they were saying rude things about Theodore Roosevelt, and the fellow—the bell captain—was injured in the Spanish War, so has an affection for Roosevelt. It was a silly war, in my opinion, but I did not share that opinion with the man, who was only serving our country.

"And, by the way, there was some argument about the hotel cigar desk not carrying a particular cigar for these men, or at least the Abe Lincoln one."

Lowell described what the cigar desk man had told him, especially that it seemed a political issue, and that one tobacconist in town, which the cigar man described by location, might carry the brand.

"We can't just wait here for Willis or his friend Davis to show up someday," Antonia said. She motioned for Elsie to please sit and pay attention. "If the cigar is our only clue, then we should follow the cigar."

"That's sensible," Lowell said. "We have a few hours before the opera, so let's have a quick sandwich here and call it dinner so that we might go to the cigar store he mentioned and see if we can learn more. I will go into that store, as such places are more comfortable with men, and he will likely talk to me in a way he will not with the two of you. We can then go to the opera from there."

Antonia fidgeted, turning her water glass around several times.

"Percival, if I may call you by your first name…" she said.

"You may both call me Percy, as do my friends."

"Percy, you have put us quite ahead of the game. But I can't have you doing my job for me. I am being paid to investigate this matter, and I must do much of it myself. Also, I should like to find dinner later so that we can go to this cigar store immediately."

"Of course. I was afraid I might be getting too much involved," he replied.

The tobacco store, its door flanked by two cigar store wooden Indians, was without customers when the three travelers entered. Antonia asked the clerk—an elderly man wearing a vest made for holding pipes and the tools of that habit—if they carried Hotel Nacional Grande cigars. The man looked surprised.

"I do carry the brand. I know of several women who smoke cigars," he said, but usually it is a daintier sort—is this for yourself?"

Antonia seemed at a loss for words, as she did not want to disclose their purpose but seemed unwilling to invent a lie.

"It is a gift for my fiancé," Elsie intervened. "We live in Arizona, but he asked us to see if we could find this brand for him, as a fellow he met at a political event gave him one and he rather liked it. Mr. Joe Willis, I believe."

"We'll take a box—wrapped, if you please," Lowell said, producing his wallet.

The counterman went to a back room and returned with the box, wrapping paper, and string.

"Mr. Willis has indeed been a regular here of late," he said as he gave Lowell his change and tied up the package. It was a half-size box, and expensive.

"Does he happen to live or work in the area?" Elsie said. "It would be nice to drop by and give him my fiancé's regards."

"I don't know miss, and sadly you just missed him by a day or so. He bought a fistful and said it would have to last him until he got back from Arizona. He was carrying a small valise, so I expect he was on his way."

It was Antonia's turn: "Elsie, is Mr. Willis the man that your fiancé said looked rather like Abe Lincoln?"

"No that was a friend of Mr. Willis's, I believe."

They let that hang in the air, which was scented by three high walls of propped-open cigar boxes.

"Davies. That would be Mr. Davies," the counterman finally let out. "Actually, I believe they met here. Robert, I believe—Robert Davies. He was coming in here every day for the last few weeks, smoking Hotel Nacional Grandes in our salon and reading two or three newspapers. Quite a nice fellow, and, yes, uncanny likeness to Lincoln from a distance. He has no beard, though, and I'm sure that saves him from gathering crowds."

"Does he live nearby?" Antonia asked.

"He is from back East, I believe, here on business, but certainly stayed long enough to be a good customer."

Lowell looked to Antonia as if for permission, but then just spoke: "We were sent here by the cigar man at the St. Francis Hotel. He mentioned that many tobacconists do not carry the brand for political reasons. I can't imagine how a cigar can be political. Do you know what he might have meant?"

"Yes, I think I do," he replied. "The cigar's paper band, as you see, features a picture of the grand hotel in Havana and a stripe of yellow and red. Those colors represent the flag of Spain, not Cuba. Cuba's flag, since the war, is red, white, and blue, as you might expect. There are many Spaniards in this city and elsewhere who would prefer that the King of Spain still ruled that island, as many family fortunes had depended on it, and Roosevelt took all of that from Spain—and the Philippines, too. If you leave the band on and are seen smoking this cigar—which in fact is produced in the Canary Islands by the King's family—you may be thought a supporter of the royalist position. At least I have heard that.

"And to be sure, the veterans of the Spanish War do not like to see these cigars, so I keep them in the back, so as not to offend anyone."

They left with the box wrapped in brown paper for travel and stopped at a pasta house, where they shared a bottle of Italian wine and a selection of bread. The manager who directed them to their table had an arm missing, and Antonia thought it was likely a souvenir from '06.

What else, or whom, did he lose that day? Don't think. This is 1911. We are in another life, another world. Good bread, finally. Moist inside, crusty out, home.

"We are getting somewhere," Antonia said. "I don't know where, but we are getting there. We have good reason to think that Buffalo Joe Willis has gone back to Arizona and may be a day or two ahead of us."

"Absolutely," Lowell said with a mouthful.

Antonia continued: "There is an evening train back to Arizona. Elsie and I should go home so we can continue the pursuit.

"Percy, thanks to you we are well on his trail. I'm now sorry you purchased the opera tickets, but this must take precedence. We need to go back. We are not here for entertainment.

"Elsie, forgive me," she continued, "I should not speak for you. I can give you a safe place to stay with my father and aunt, and you and Dr. Lowell can see the opera. I know you have always wanted to see one."

"Thank you, Antonia," Elsie replied, "but I want to see this through. I want to see Agnes's killer caught and it would mean the world to me if I could help you do that. I will see an opera someday."

"Ladies," Lowell said as he raised his wine glass as if for a toast, "I'm sure the bell captain can find people who very much want to go to that opera, although I must tell you that this city still waits for a new opera house worth attending. The old one, before the big shake—my god, was that five years ago already?—was absolutely perfect. Anyway, tonight's performance is a Puccini, a favorite in this town, so tickets will be in high demand. I suggest we return to the hotel forthwith and pack our bags."

"Why would you want to go with us, Percy?" Antonia asked. "You have that camera thing to receive."

"I shall wire him. He can leave it in the care of the Astronomical Society of the Pacific, whose offices are here. They arranged his expedition, in fact. You can send wires to ships now, did you know? —at least some ships. The Society can hold it until my next trip here. I shall accompany you because it will be exciting and because I rather like my new charitable work in the field of justice. I think we know that you came with a very limited budget. I shall see that you have a compartment on the train home and that you have anything else you need, at least in the material sense. I will go with you all the way to Phoenix and still be back in Flagstaff in time for a solar transit of Venus, which is the only important item on my calendar for some weeks. And, by the way, we shall need two hotel rooms in Ash Fork, as we will be arriving there tomorrow night and the train south from there, to Prescott and Phoenix, does not come through until the next morning. On your budget, you will otherwise be sleeping in the ladies' room at the train station. You really do need me to travel respectably, you know."

Lowell nearly offered the box of cigars to the waiter, but then thought better of it. "These may come in handy at some point," he said to Antonia. "You may want to dangle them on a hook and see who lights them up."

"Antonia is good at baiting hooks," Elsie said. "I'll keep hold of them for her.".

Antonia packed the gowns for transit back to her aunt and slipped in a note, while Elsie looked out the high hotel window at a city she would have to explore another time. Construction crews were everywhere on every block. Only a few lots were still piled with brick rubble where great buildings once stood. The sound of hammers and machinery and rivet guns, mixed with the calls of seagulls in the bright blue above her, could be heard through the glass. She could see the bay and its sailboats and ferries and cargo boats and sparkling French curves of wind on the water as if in a painting come to life.

"So beautiful. The people are so beautiful, too," she said, "And so many of them. You could be anything you wanted in a place like this. Everything is starting over."

The train departed from the Third and Townsend station a few minutes before midnight. At San Jose, most passengers were already reading in their bunks. After the big turn at Lathrop, the train picked up speed toward Merced and Fresno, with the distant Sierras visible by moonlight.

The three investigators conversed late in the club car. The night steward brought a small bottle of cognac and three glasses.

"Have you come across this Arthur Conan Doyle fellow, the author of mysteries?" Lowell asked Antonia and Elsie.

"You mean the Sherlock Holmes stories," answered Elsie. "I have read some of his short ones, not the big books."

"Exactly the character," Lowell said. "I propose we take this quiet moment to consider the clues that we now have before us. Antonia, you are Holmes. I am Dr. Watson, the half-witted companion. You, Miss Cork, are the chief of Scotland Yard. You and I, dear, are always a step behind Holmes."

"I am satisfied with that," Elsie said, "for now."

Another passenger came in and was standing in the gloom at the far end, perhaps listening, but then came nearer. He was seen first by Lowell, who appeared shocked. The women, too, could now see a man who well might play Lincoln on stage.

"You are all up rather late. I was going to have a cigar, but I shall…"

"No, no. Have your smoke, sir. We are just now retiring to our compartments," Lowell said. They rose and departed, with Lowell grabbing the cognac and the small glasses. In brushing past the man, Lowell saw a fat cigar protruding from the handkerchief pocket of his coat, with its bright yellow and red band displayed for anyone to see—the band of a Hotel Nacional Grande.

Lowell followed the women into their compartment.

"Well, well," he said, as he clicked a fold-down table into place to make their bar.

"This is too much of a coincidence," he said, "which, I must say, is always the weakness of a

Holmes story. I feel like the dog who has caught the wheel of a carriage and is spinning around with it."

Elsie took a great breath: "Tomorrow, I am certain I can get lots of information from him. Men can get very talkative and sure of themselves in my care."

"You shall do no such thing—no such seduction, please," Antonia scolded. "He is partners with a man who wants you dead. We have no idea if he knows who we are. He may be on this train because we are. We must be terribly cautious."

"All right," Elsie replied, "but if I might say, seduction is too grand a word for the capture of any man; they can be had with a wink."

"We should get some rest," Lowell said, "and I should not be in your compartment. But let's take a moment to consider our clues, so that we may let our dreams work on them while we sleep," He poured three small drinks, arranging the glasses as if pawns on the table's printed chessboard.

Elsie moved them each to the royal edge.

"You need to think better of us," she said.

Antonia described how, the previous day, her friend Roscoe McNary had argued for a connection between the McKinley assassination and Buffalo Joe. Elsie explained how her friend, Agnes Bailey, had overheard someone mention that Buffalo Joe did it, and that had got her killed.

"Remarkable," Lowell replied. "Let us assume for a moment that this Buffalo Joe Willis fellow, wherever he is at present, did indeed have some involvement with the McKinley tragedy, as your old friend claimed. The question would be *why?* Buffalo

Joe is a rancher and a dealer in ranches and mines; he is not some anarchist trying to bring down all men of power. But history knows, or thinks it knows, that McKinley was shot by an anarchist, and one described as a crazy fellow. Now, surely, a crazy fellow could be encouraged to do such a thing and could be put in the right place to do it, rather like a wind-up walking toy, but why would a successful Arizona man even want to do that?"

"To get Theodore Roosevelt into the White House," Antonia said. "That's what Roscoe said— and to thereby gain water and statehood for Arizona."

"The thing is," Elsie offered, "getting statehood seems like something nice that you might want, but not enough to kill for. It doesn't sound quite right."

"That's exactly what the Rough Riders killed and died for, according to Roscoe," Antonia replied.

"They will also kill for water," Lowell said. "They will ever so more happily kill for water. There was a lot of money—big fortunes—at stake ten years ago, exactly in regard to Arizona water. A friend of mine who grew up back East and now has a great deal of farmland around Phoenix tried very hard to get Congress—and he has those connections—to use federal money to set up an irrigation system in Arizona to stop the floods and provide controlled water year-round. Well, Congress wasn't having it, but as soon as Teddy got into the White House, that bill sailed through, and Teddy signed it.

"Now, my friend Dwight is a good man and would never have anything to do with the killing of a president. But he isn't the usual sort for Arizona. He's a Massachusetts fellow, like me. He owns a big enterprise—land and cattle and other businesses in Arizona. His wife has money. He's not going to do something foolish. But, as I said, he's not the usual sort. There's still a strain of the Tombstone gunslinger and the claim jumper and the ambusher in Arizona, and some of these fellows are in politics and business now. So, for argument, let's say they did send someone like Joe Willis off to Buffalo to take care of McKinley. Where does that leave us?"

"And why would a Taft man in San Francisco want to deal with him these ten years later?" Antonia asked.

"You know," Elsie said, "I would bet you a dollar the whole federal government knows who was behind the killing of McKinley. They investigate everything to death. Maybe the man who was in the White House when they figured it out decided to keep the blame on the anarchists and keep the killer in a back pocket for future use."

"You're quite cynical," Antonia said. "And just what would they want to take him out of their pocket and use him for?"

"Well, if the killer ended up in Taft's pocket, Taft hates Teddy, doesn't he—or his political people do?" Elsie replied. "They don't want him running against Taft, right? And, with the dam dedication coming up, Roosevelt is heading to Arizona and so is Willis. It sounds mad, but now that we've seen some of the pieces and how they're moving on the board, maybe it isn't."

"Teddy Roosevelt is the most popular man in America," Lowell said. "If he wants to take the nomination away from Taft, I imagine he can do it. So, yes, assuming the very darkest of intentions, Willis may be on his way to kill Teddy, and Abe Lincoln here may be on his way to help him."

To best dramatize the moment, a desert thunderstorm made a show of lightning and a spray of rain against the windows.

"It's a decent working hypothesis," Lowell replied, turning his attention to the weather.

"A working hippopotamus?" Elsie asked.

"It just means it's a reasonable possibility— something to go on, at least until we know better," he explained.

"I know. I was being funny."

Antonia was still standing and fidgeting.

"I don't think I can share all this with my boss, the coroner, or the sheriff in Prescott. I don't know who knows what. Whom can we trust on this?"

"Well," answered Lowell, "believe it or not, I think we can trust my land-owning friend Dwight in Phoenix. When we get to Needles in the morning, I'll wire my girl and have her see if Dwight can meet us in Phoenix with some resources."

"If you don't mind my saying so," Elsie said, "he seems like one of the last people we should trust. And your girl? Do you mean your daughter? Or possibly your wife?"

"No, not Constance, my wife. Constance is busy with a thousand things. My girl is Wrexie Leonard. She is my secretary and all that. Very competent and an indispensable companion at the telescope each night and for special projects, as when we traveled to Africa to look for an observatory site."

"Indispensable, I'm sure," Elsie said. "I'm sure all that telescope-looking must go quite late into the night. I, too, would someday like both a husband and a boy who is indispensable."

"You are embarrassing me."

"You deserve it, Nursey Percy. Do you have other mistresses, too? Will you wire me if there is an opening?"

Lowell flushed red, looked down, and refilled the three glasses.

"Anyway," Lowell said, "Dwight is a gentleman, and we can trust him. I'll put my life on that. He will open the right doors for us. We must now plan for tomorrow and then get some rest."

"Percy, do you know how to handle a gun?" Antonia asked.

"Certainly."

She fished out from her bag a small revolver she had collected before leaving Prescott, thinking Elsie might need something.

"Let's be careful tonight," she said as she handed it to him. "No opening doors unless we know who's knocking. We'll meet in the dining car, say at eight, and talk only about auto cars. If this Abe Lincoln engages us in conversation and asks us almost anything that might trip us up, we're traveling to a sad funeral in Phoenix, and we really don't want to talk about it."

"May we cry?" Elsie asked. "By the way, Mike Wall—we could trust Mike, you know."

Antonia nodded.

Lowell said he didn't know the man and so would have no opinion. He took a last swig of cognac before retiring to his own compartment. All doors were secured. Both compartments contained a loaded steel revolver rattling on a steel table.

"Did you have to go to school to learn to do what you do?" Elsie asked in the dark.

"I did."

"Well, I guess that makes sense. I mean, you are a medical woman—but one that certainly doesn't have to worry about doing harm to her patients."

"Why do you ask?"

"Oh, I don't know. I mean, I'd like to be like you. My line of work doesn't last very long and I'm not immune to the shame of it. But I could never afford medical school, and they wouldn't let me in, anyway–not with my background. But maybe I could be a detective of some sort, without the medical part?"

"You might have to get some training for that if you want to be respected as a detective. Some states require you to pass a test and carry a badge, even as a private one. But you could do that. Having a colorful history might even be seen as a benefit to that work."

"I'm going to think on all that. I really appreciate your friendship and how you and Dr. Lowell don't talk down to me, at least to my face."

"Elsie, we would never speak ill of you behind your back. You are a valuable member of our little team."

Antonia could hear Elsie weeping softly in the bunk above her, but then she stopped abruptly, leaving only the rhythmic click of the tracks below.

"Tell me about the earthquake!" Elsie said, leaning down to look at Antonia through the dark. "I heard you tell Dr. Lowell that you grew up in San Francisco with your parents and baby sister. I want to know what the earthquake was like for you and your family. I know you lost some of them. I know it must have been awful."

8. All Muscle and Smoke

Five years earlier, on the morning of the earthquake, nineteen-year-old Antonia, wearing a white nurse's dress, was on a passenger ferryboat starting across San Francisco Bay toward Oakland. It was crowded with workers from the tenements of the city, heading to jobs in the stores, schools, factories, and shipyards of the burgeoning East Bay.

After schooling at an Oakland convent school, she had recently completed training as a nurse at Oakland's Fabiola Hospital and was now earning her first income. Her intention was to gain a recommendation sufficient to secure a position in San Francisco proper.

It was dawn. The ferryboat was but a few minutes out from the San Francisco wharf when, at 5:13, it began to rock violently, as if a great but invisible ocean liner had suddenly passed too near.

The ferry's captain cut the engines. Passengers began looking back at the periwinkle-domed skyline of the city, where great dust clouds now appeared in every quarter. And then a deep, rolling roar was heard from the city, with high notes from the screams of a whole population—almost like a cheer, as if a thousand athletic teams had made great scores in a thousand ballparks. But when the highest buildings could be seen to sway, and when their facades and cornices could be seen crumbling and falling, the fact of the moment became clear, and the word *earthquake* raced like sheet lightning through the ferry's crowd. Men stood petrified, their fingers locked into their mustaches; women dug their fingers into the arms of nearby women passengers or held their hands to their mouths to muffle screams, and then whispered *dear God, dear God* as rosaries to calm themselves.

"Go back!" came as a call from the passengers to the crew. "We have our families back there!" one man shouted above the others.

The ferry bobbed in the water for a few minutes before the captain shouted on three places throughout the ship that he would indeed return to San Francisco as a precaution because earthquakes sometimes produce tidal waves. The passengers applauded him and called for him to be quick about it. "His family is probably there, too," a woman said to Antonia.

When they reached the pier, so many were clustered for a rushed exit that the boat seemed in danger of tipping into the still choppy waters. Antonia was locked in the nervous crush and was nearly ejected onto the wooden wharf when the ship's gates swung open. The crowd dispersed in every crumbling direction, while Antonia and perhaps fifty others ran straight up Market Street.

The buildings of that street were falling with each new shock and were now beginning to burn from broken gas mains. Pieces of fallen cement columns rolled by, and half-dressed people screamed in the street while others shoveled through bricks with their bare hands, either to free themselves or in search of the ones they loved. Every face seemed bloodied, every eye wide and mouth open. The pavement was so fractured by faults that she had to jump over many, though they were still shifting and growing. She passed the grand Chronicle newspaper building, now a shell, as were the Call and Examiner offices.

She could hear people crying for help from rubble everywhere, but she was determined to complete the eleven blocks to her family's top-floor apartment in the three-story Newton. The Post Office at Market and Seventh was gone. The heat was intense as she ran.

Buildings were becoming engulfed in tornadoes of orange gas flames that now found timbers and walls and furniture and the bodies of victims, some still alive enough to scream.

She shielded her face from intense heat as it flared up on her left and right. She spun around and turned to walk backward several times when there was too much heat directly ahead.

Many street signs were buried now in rubble, but she kept her bearings in this diorama of tragedy by counting the side streets and looking for landmarks. Finally, the ruins of what must be the great Majestic Theater and the Adventist Church loomed in view through dust and smoke.

The street rolled beneath her again and again as the shocks continued, each sending a new load of bricks and carved stones and gargoyles and timbers and steel beams crashing down on what used to be sidewalks. Each came also with fresh screams and scurrying, as those who desperately knelt, casting away bricks in hopes of finding their loves, ran for a moment into the middle of Market Street and then returned to the impossible mounds, always shouting the names of those they sought. Many called to her for help: "Nurse, over here!" and the like, owing to her dress, which was now hardly white. But she kept going toward her own family.

She braved the interior of the Majestic, as her father often worked there at dawn to prepare Italian desserts for the great bar in the lobby. She believed he was more likely across town, having lately been an outdoor night watchman at one of Golden Gate Park's museums.

But she wanted to be sure. She entered the Majestic, calling his name. The acoustics of the great new theater, home to operas and plays and concerts, were now ruined. Her shouts, in a drama more real than anything that had come from the stage, passed the two shattered and hanging balconies and continued up through the fallen ceiling and roof, revealing the airy red cauldron of San Francisco's sky.

"Father!" she called. "Tony Bonaventura!" she called out, just as another roll of the earth sent plaster down around her. He was not there or else was too deep in heaps of debris for help.

She picked her way carefully out and returned to the heat of Market Street, which she crossed and was finally at the Newton. It was still standing but at an angle. It was a wood building, an advantage in an earthquake, but the brick buildings on either side had crashed into it and through it. The Newton's two front doors were on the sidewalk, having been popped off their hinges and out of their frames by the tilt of the beams.

The stairway was deep in plaster and bricks, but she bounded to the second floor. There were no calls for help from anywhere in the building. She glanced through the open apartment door of newspaperman Jerry Carroll and his wife Gladys—close family friends. There was no sign of the couple.

"Mother! Agnes Marie!" she called as she rose to the third floor.

The apartment door was standing open.

The main room and kitchen walls were open to the half-collapsed building next door. The sink was hanging out the side and water was dripping from its pipes. Antonia's own room was to the right, but she went first to the left, to little Agnes's room—almost a closet off the kitchen with an Irish curtain for a door. She stepped inside.

Agnes, two years old, was buried under bricks that had crashed through a wall and window. The child was half under a little bed that had not saved her. Antonia furiously removed bricks and splintered wood until she could see Agnes's lifeless face, eyes open in terror. She lifted her to her breast and hugged her.

Then, "Mommy!" she called to the next room, to no answer. She kissed the dead child's bloodied face and carried her with her, weeping so madly that her back arched and her eyes rolled back and her legs turned leaden, but she continued on, stumbling back through the kitchen to her parents' room.

Her mother was under a greater avalanche of bricks and plaster, on a bed that was broken to the floor by the weight. She set down Agnes's body in a corner and began throwing bricks and debris aside. She found her mother's face and knew she was dead. She kissed her mother on the lips, as their family always did.

She then saw an arm that didn't belong there. Was her father also in the bed? She threw off more debris.

It was Mr. Donofrio, who lived in the next apartment. He was dead.

"Mr. Donofrio! Why are you here?" she asked his torn face.

"This won't do, Mr. Donofrio," she said. She grabbed his feet and pulled him free of the last bricks. He was in a nightshirt that was insufficient to cover him as she pulled. She stopped every few pulls to make him decent as she slid him across the brick-strewn floor, delivering him to the landing outside his own apartment.

She heard a man down on the first floor, yelling up the stairwell that the building would soon be burning, and anyone still inside should get out quickly. The smoke was thickening, and she could feel the heat from the collapsed building next door.

Her mother was in a nightshirt. Antonia found a large blanket in the bedroom closet and laid it out over bricks so that she could roll her mother onto it. She then took little Agnes and put the two of them in the blanket together, rolling it and securing it with three of her father's belts.

In the closet, she had seen the tattered sheaf of her father's poems—a hundred or so that were a family treasure: some in Italian, some translated into English, some written in his new English. She stuffed the sheaf into a canvas shopping tote retrieved from her own room and slung it over her back.

She then dragged her dead family down the stairs in the blanket roll and then out the front door, where she rolled her load onto one of the doors and dragged it as a litter to the middle of Market Street. She looked up to see the third floor exploding in flames.

"We're all right now, my darlings," she heard herself say.

A man of perhaps fifty years was sitting near her in the street. "They're gone. They're all gone," he said to Antonia. He gestured toward the collapsed and flaming building next door that, falling, had also doomed Antonia's loved ones.

"I am so terribly sorry," she said. "But could you help me, sir?"

His head jerked as if he had come out of a trance. He stood up and dusted himself off to the extent possible. His hands and his head were burned and bleeding.

"Delighted!" he said, as though it were any fine morning.

"Where shall I take my family?" she asked. "I have them here. I got them out."

"Well, now," he answered, "I hear people shouting they must get to Golden Gate Park or the Presidio—open ground, I suppose. Just a minute ago a woman told me I should go to Mechanics Pavilion, as it's just a few blocks away and is built like a fort. And I guess that's right, too. But I may stay here for a while."

"Could you help me carry them?" Antonia asked of him.

"I need to stay here. I can't leave my family…just yet." He looked around and suddenly seemed pleased with an idea. "Maybe I can fix something up for you," he said. "I'm rather good at that, my wife says—said."

He had spotted a baby carriage. It was ruined, but he pulled the wheel assembly free of it with easy strength. He set the wheels under the door so that, with care, Antonia might move the litter down the street like a barrow. Then, and again with strength that surprised Antonia, he ripped the two rope edges from a mattress lying in the street and used them to bind wheels, door, and load together.

"There, quite fancy. I wish you good luck, miss."

She moved the barrow along Market toward Ninth, where a turn north would get her to Mechanics Pavilion. She looked back and saw that the man who had helped her was sitting again, but bent over forward to the pavement in a pose of death. Probably his heart, she thought, though, if he shot himself, she knew she would not have heard it over the roar of destruction. She was hearing many gunshots, or perhaps snapping timbers or bricks falling onto tin. Many in San Francisco carried pistols as a matter of course, especially in the hard neighborhoods along Market—the Tenderloin, as it was called.

She took a last look at the Majestic. It had been so grand. Her father loved working there and was permitted to stand in the back to hear evening concerts. He had written a little poem of appreciation and put it in the dressing room of an Italian conductor:

The maestro's poised baton
Stops our thousand breaths
Cocks-back-our-hearts!

He had introduced Antonia to the conductor when helping her find a summer job in the theater. She repeated the poem several times as she worried about where her father might be and if he would please still be among the living. For an instant she thought about how she had never told her father—and never would—how the conductor had treated her.

She returned to saying Hail Marys under her scorched breath and she moved on.

The street was now an oven of fires, and the survivors were stumbling around, some calling for help and some calling for water to put out the fires in their own throats. Antonia kept losing her grip, but she continued pushing and pulling the barrow through the heat and debris. She turned on Ninth and saw Mechanics Pavilion. Its architectural towers and flourishes had sloughed away as if from a sandcastle, but the main part was standing and seemed a strong refuge. She pushed her cart into the massive hall. Two dozen people were kneeling and praying in the center of a floor large enough for the polo games often held there.

She wheeled her barrow into an alcove that she thought must be for the storage of chairs—thousands of chairs were set out in the pavilion for some event that would not happen. The alcove seemed a little chapel for her purpose.

Her intention now would be to find her father and to find out where she should take the bodies of her family. But first, she sat in one of the folding chairs and tried to cry. She could not. She was terribly thirsty and shaking. The heat, she realized, had taken all the water from her and there was nothing left for tears.

Our Father who art in Heaven...

She started that prayer aloud but then stopped because it might be unlucky for her earthly father, and so went back to the Hail Marys.

She wandered back into the entrance lobby and found a drinking fountain that provided a few drops. There was a refreshment bar that must have something. She found six unopened little cans of condensed milk and carried them back to the barrow, where her shoulder bag was still resting on one corner. In it were a few dollars, a comb and mirror, a notebook, and her father's poems.

For the first time since leaving the ferry, she looked down at herself. Her dress was now mostly gray and black. The hem on her left side seemed scorched, though she didn't remember stepping through coals or fire. She then noticed that her left hand was in pain as if from a burn—likely from spanking out the flames on her dress. She sat down to gather herself before whatever might come next.

"Miss Bonaventura!" she heard a voice call out. She turned to see the silhouette of a young man standing in a doorway and calling to her.

"Is that you, Miss Bonaventura?"

She stood.

It took her a few moments to place him: Dr. William John Walsh, who made weekly teaching rounds at her hospital in Oakland and was the twenty-six-year-old elected coroner of San Francisco City and County. He had always looked interesting to her: tall, dark-haired, small mouth and chin, but with neither mustache nor beard, setting him apart from most other men, especially those of small chin. She once overheard him say to other young physicians that he thought facial hair on a doctor was an unnecessary sanitation risk for patients.

"Oh, Doctor Walsh! How are you, sir? So nice to see you. I'm sorry, that sounds insane. Hello, Doctor Walsh. How awful this is, but I am very glad to see someone I know still alive."

"So am I, Miss Bonaventura, so am I."

He sat down beside her and noticed the improvised cart in the alcove nearby.

"Who is that?" he asked.

"Most of my family, sir. I am hoping to yet find my father alive."

"I pray for you and for him. And for them, Miss Bonaventura. And, as you are here, I think I need to ask for your assistance. My deputy is missing. I don't know if he is alive. I know you are a very good nurse. Might I engage you as my special volunteer today?"

She nodded.

"Here's our situation. An Army general and federal troops have taken over the city, as is proper, and Mayor Schmitz, within the hour, will declare that the soldiers will shoot looters on the spot. No one will be allowed into the city from across the Bay or from the south. The power and gas and water are now mostly off, and the water mains are gone. I have established several temporary morgues, especially one at the main Police Station, and put police and soldiers in charge for now, but most are in the path of the fires, and bodies are being temporarily moved to Portsmouth Square. I am here in this building to see if it will do for a main morgue and a place where the injured can be treated. We need something in this area. Most of the damage is in this part of the city. I think this will do."

"Any care will be difficult without water," Antonia said.

"Indeed. Barrels of it are now being sent over on the ferryboats, as they return after shipping thousands and thousands of people to the East Bay cities—there is quite a panic to get out. We should have water soon, at least some. I shall get some soldiers to break into some drug stores for supplies and bring them here. Only they can do that and not be shot—also some mattresses and sheets and whatnot from any stores they see. It will all burn, anyway."

"What should I do?"

"Organize this place to the extent you can. For example, reserve the right side of the Pavilion for the dead, and the left side for the injured. Remove most of these chairs. Recruit volunteers. I will send cots and nurses within an hour or two, assuming I can get the cooperation of the Army's man in charge, General Funston, and I think I can. He has doctors and nurses at the Presidio, and some will be sent to me here with some troops. The Central Emergency Hospital, across the street, is ruined, as I'm sure you saw, but most of its staff is alive. Many of them, if their families don't need them, will report for duty to move any surviving patients here from their hospital, as that building will surely burn. Other doctors and nurses are coming on the ferries from hospitals across the way. Can I count on you to ready this hall?"

"Of course," Antonia said, standing up as she spoke. They shook bloody hands.

"And your family?" she remembered to ask. "You are newly married."

"Yes, Jane is fine. Thank you. I put her on a ferry first thing. Her family is in Berkeley."

"Good. I'm so very glad—and so you think this building is safe, then?"

"Nothing is safe but our resolve," he replied with a nod and a stiff smile, then going quickly on his way.

"There's a fine man," she whispered aloud to her charges. "Dear Mother, darling Agnes, are your spirits still here? Did you hear Dr. Walsh? I have some work to do now. I will be nearby. I love you both so much!"

Antonia interrupted the gathering of people who were praying and told them what needed to be done, her tattered nurse's dress giving her sufficient authority in their eyes. Under her direction, more than a thousand chairs were folded and stacked here and there. Two rows of unfolded chairs were placed to create a long center aisle through the pavilion, separating the coming living from the coming dead. To keep records, paper and pencils were found in the pavilion's office that two men broke open for her.

Dozens of six-foot tables were set up on the living side where they might be used as desks and operating tables and to hold bandages and other supplies including food and water if God and the Army might so provide.

Word spread quickly through the city, and survivors limped in or were carried in by family members and friends—and they also carried in the dead. Antonia counted fifty-three injured but living children before the Army arrived with cots and materials and finally a crew of doctors and nurses.

By the time Coroner Walsh returned, the Pavilion was essentially the front-line hospital of a war, the enemies being nature and architecture. Antonia was still in charge of much of what was happening, and the last white of her dress was gone to red. Behind Walsh through the door came eight soldiers with four water barrels that raised a hoarse cheer from many inside.

Dr. Charles Millar, the chief surgeon of the fallen Emergency Hospital across the street, arrived to take charge of the living.

Coroner Walsh returned several hours later and made a tour of the building, where sports and speeches had recently prevailed, and then pulled Antonia aside and sat her down.

"There's more water coming," he told her. "I'm sorry it's so late. As soon as barrels have been coming off the ferries, thirsty mobs have been attacking and taking them and breaking them open. Most of the water is lost this way, but we have soldiers now meeting the ferries and some will bring more water here. The city is a damned oven, and this building will soon burn, too," he said.

"It's brick," she replied.

"Yes, but the fires are like great storms. They bake everything in their path. I'm looking for enough wagons to get these people to the Presidio or Golden Gate Park. Those who can walk will need to walk. So, we need to do something else, now."

Antonia nodded. She was ready to do anything.

"I need you to get some stalwart volunteers and examine the dead for anything that might give identification. Some have names pinned on them by friends and relatives, of course, but others do not, yet may have something, even laundry marking on their clothes or a locket with someone's picture or an engraved watch or ring, that will give us something relatives might identify. So do that, and make a rough identification of each person, including race, age, height, approximate weight, identifying marks, if possible, and whatever might help relatives have some peace when this is over. So many will just disappear, and people will not know for certain if they are gone. So, this is important work. Can you do it?"

"We will evacuate only the living? We are leaving the dead behind?" she asked.

"We will have to. There are more than two-hundred dead here and no way to move them without leaving some of the living behind. I would say we have an hour. Do what you can."

"My own family…" she said, pointing to the improvised cart in the alcove.

"My darling young lady," he replied, "you must think of this hard day as a Second Coming. The city itself is a crematorium now. Spirits are rising to Heaven from this place. You may be certain that, if there be after-spirits, yours surely know and feel the love in your heart for them as you send them home."

Walsh placed his hands on her shoulders and then turned to leave, but then spun around.

"You know a newspaperman named Jerry something?"

"Jerry Carroll, yes, a neighbor."

"He has been dogging me for hours for the Associated Press, I believe."

"Yes, that's him. He's all right?"

"His wife was injured but not seriously. He seems fine. For his reporting, I mentioned you by name as my acting assistant and what you are doing over here, and he was delighted to hear that you are well. And here is the thing: he has seen your father. I'm quite sure he said that. Your father may be all right and praying that you are all right."

After that shock of joy that made her weep, she began the hurried work with five women volunteers to inventory the dead.

By noon, the count was over five-hundred injured and over four-hundred dead. Antonia, for the second time, moved the center aisle to make more space for the living, with some of the dead stacked upon one another, after having been examined and notes taken.

The light was dim, the great windows admitted only the rosy light of surrounding fires. The wail of the grieving and the grievously injured was nearly deafening and constant, much coming from operating tables where the injured, including those with burns and lacerations and broken bones that protruded from skin, were treated without anesthetic.

At less than an hour after noon, when the storm of fire was but a half-block away, the last of the living were carried or escorted out to Army wagons and any available vehicles or to walk beside them through the heat to Golden Gate Park.

As they passed through the safer parts of the city, many of the less injured were taken into private homes in countless acts of kindness.

The last of the living to leave Mechanics Pavilion was Antonia. She kissed the bundle of her loved ones and said goodbye. She took only her shoulder bag containing the documents describing as many of the dead as could be determined, plus her own few things, her mother's wedding ring, little Agnes's holy necklace, and her father's poetry.

She would find him in Golden Gate Park the next day. They both had slept in the Army's tents but far apart until they saw each other in a food line.

An earthquake camp in San Francisco

That evening, in a tent by flickering electric bulb, she read him some of his own poems, but not the lovely ones that he had written to Antonia's mother. She found instead some that took broader themes:

Into your velvet coves
North America we came
By force—such an invasion!
Our sail and steamboats teeming
Our endless ships hustling up
Your Chesapeake
Your Hudson, your Delaware
All muscle and smoke
Your Albemarle, Charleston Bay
Mobile, Mississippi!
Into Puget Sound we came
Into San Francisco Bay
We tired, poor, chained,
Dreaming, anxious, peering
For centuries now
And still streaming!

"That's a pretty good one," he agreed. "That's who we are, isn't it?"

The next day, after failing to find her father's sister on Castro Street, they walked the ten miles south to Millbrae, where her father had a rich poet friend, Mr. Mills, with an estate house. They walked in the hope that the town was all right, and, but for a brick powerhouse, it was. She read her father a few of his own poems along the walk, including ones he wrote for her childhood.

In the last minutes of Mechanics Pavilion, Coroner Walsh had asked her to continue her work with him, as it was just getting started, he said. Therefore, two days later, via the trains that had returned to service, she and her father arrived back in the city. She first located her father's sister and settled him there, then reported for work at the improvised city hall.

Antonia told as much of this to Elsie as might give an outline of the experience. She decided Elsie was likely asleep when she told some of the story, but as she finished, Elsie's hand came down from her bunk in the dim light of the compartment and waved for Antonia to grasp it, which she did.

"I'm sure you didn't tell your father about the neighbor. But, honestly Antonia, he was probably there to rescue the family. That's why the door was open."

"That's what I'm thinking," Antonia answered.

"But I have to ask: Baby Agnes was quite a late-life baby for your folks, wasn't she?"

"Yes."

"Antonia, was she truly your sister? Was she instead your own child?"

Antonia paused a long moment before answering and held firm to Elsie's hand.

"She was. She was my little girl, Agnes Marie, and I left her in the Pavilion to burn, and my mother, too."

"She would have had such a lovely life, with you as her mother. I'm so very sorry."

Elsie's voice cracked a little in saying that, and she continued in a whisper that had something of a breathy melody to it that put Antonia in mind of a pan flute.

"And honestly, Antonia, you had no choice in leaving them there. It was a Second Coming my friend, like the doctor told you. Their spirits abide in you. You must let them be joyful. It is a miracle for any of us to be alive for even an hour. It is God's good grace that some of us die in a moment or an hour instead of drawn-out in old age or illness. Anyway, their spirits know you held them in that hour. I do believe that. Do you, my Catholic friend? Of course, all we can do is hope."

"I do hope."

"We do. We simply must," Elsie said.

"I don't know why people die," Antonia said, almost in anger.

Elsie gave a little dark laugh.

"What was that?" Antonia asked.

"I'm sorry. I shouldn't have laughed. You said you don't know why people die, and it occurred to me you have made a career of that question."

"I suppose that's true. And you don't have to apologize for thinking that. And, Elsie, I have put you in danger to get this far. Thank you, but you needn't stay with me in this venture. You have done your part."

"Listen, Antonia, I am in this until Buffalo Joe is dead, all right? I knew Agnes Bailey since our orphanage days. I got her into this ugly business. I'm settling her account.

~

9. Making Omelets

Spanish omelets, easy to make in the train kitchen, were aggressively recommended by the waiters of the dining car, and the three travelers accepted. The great and empty expanse of the Mojave Desert was slipping by in browns and greens.

"I generally don't trust ham dishes, but this was superb," Lowell pronounced to his companions and the steward as the dishes were taken.

They retired to the club car, sitting several tables away from their prey, who was alone, watching the moving landscape.

"Do you know what you have to do to make an omelet?" Elsie asked her mates.

"I sense that you are about to show us," Lowell said.

"I am," she replied, standing and pulling a Hotel Nacional Grande cigar from her purse. "This is how it is done." She walked the dozen steps to the man who looked like Lincoln and stood at his table until he rose like a gentleman.

"Do you have a light, sir?" she said, letting the cigar pass into her lips up to its red and yellow band.

The chatter in the car, the collection of dishes and silver, and the click of the rails did not allow Antonia and Lowell to overhear the conversation as Davies lit her cigar, lit one of his own, and offered her to please sit in conversation. That much could be seen by Antonia, and she described it to Lowell so that he needn't turn around and stare.

"Did you ask her to do that?" Lowell asked.

"Not at all—not at all; I am horrified."

"As am I," Lowell replied, "but she is right about making omelets—that's how it is done. Exactly so." He could not suppress a chuckle. Antonia shook her head and closed her eyes.

Davies motioned to Elsie's cigar: "Nice cigar, miss. I favor that cigar myself, as you can see."

Elsie smiled and took a small drag of it.

"I am told the king of Spain prefers them," he said, "and his followers, as well. But you hear so many things about the lore of cigars."

"I suppose so," she answered.

"I was just trying to remember the king's name…" he trailed off so that she might finish for him."

"I believe it's Alfonso. Maybe the thirteenth?"

"That sounds right," Davies said, settling into a smile. "I must assume that you admire him if you know his name."

"He is a king. I favor strong men generally," she answered. "And I favor nations that mind their own business."

"What is the nature of your journey, miss, if I may ask?"

"We are rather on a funeral trip, of a sort. Nothing that I would prefer to talk about if you don't mind."

"Not at all. Are you a San Franciscan, miss?"

"Sacramento."

"Ah, famous for its tomatoes."

"Thank you, sir. Do you enjoy tomatoes?" She stared at him unblinking, waiting for his reply.

"May I introduce myself?" he finally stuttered.

"Please don't. But do let us talk for a little while. Perhaps someone will introduce us later."

"As you wish, miss. May I ask how or where you happened across my favorite brand of cigar?"

"A friend, but he might not want my mentioning his name."

"I appreciate your discretion."

"I am the soul of that, sir."

"I am shy about filling a car with my smoke. Now that there are two of us with bold cigars, perhaps we should get some air? —that is if your friends would not miss you," he said.

"I barely know those people," she answered.

"Really! I assumed it was your sister and an uncle."

"They are, but I barely know them, and they don't approve of my smoking."

Davies laughed and stood up and gave her a hand; she took it, stood, and looked back to wink at Antonia, who was frowning and firmly shaking her head no. Davies smiled at Antonia and Lowell as they passed to the windy vestibule between their car and the next.

They took in the wind, and Elsie motioned to the beauty of the desert.

"Yes, lovely," he replied. "Let's go a bit farther back," Davies said, pointing to the next car.

"I'll not be going to your compartment, sir," Elsie said, almost in her Irish.

"No, we're just going for the best air. We're still breathing more smoke from the engine than from our cigars. Let's keep going."

They continued through Pullmans and the kitchen and a baggage car full of strapped and buckled suitcases and trunks and were finally looking across the last coupling to a bright yellow caboose.

"I think this is as far as we are allowed to go," Elsie said.

"Let's keep going. I'm sure the crew won't mind—they're busy elsewhere, I'm sure," he answered.

The caboose was outfitted with several steel beds, a small Franklin stove, a kitchen and a bathroom of sorts, and a small ladder leading up to a cupola where an elevated seat gave a forward and rear view of the train. Schedules and various posters regarding rules and safety were pasted to every wall.

"We'll keep going," he insisted. They continued to the windy back vestibule.

"You are right. It's nice back here," Elsie said as they settled against the rail at the very rear of the train. "You could make a good speech from here," she said, but we mustn't stay long, or my friends will worry."

"They are your friends now, not family?"

She looked and smiled but did not answer.

"Actually, I do want to make a little speech." He said, "and I wanted this privacy so I might ask you a few questions."

His expression now seemed to her quite serious, and he had moved closer, almost crowding her into a rounded corner of the railing. She looked down to see the blur of the railbed below.

"Are you heading to Phoenix, by chance?" he asked.

She smiled but did not answer.

"I ask because there's a big thing about to happen in Phoenix. Do you know about it?" Again, she smiled but did not answer.

"Fine," he said, "but when we are formally introduced, perhaps you will talk more freely with me. But let me ask you a last question. When Roosevelt was president, how did you feel about him? Did you like him?"

"I don't care one way or another about politicians. They can live or die, as far as I'm concerned. I stay out of politics. It's for men and is bad for friendships and can be dangerous."

"Indeed, it can be," he replied. "Would you let me show you something? I'll want to fetch something from my compartment. Will you wait here for me? It's important."

"All right," was all she could think to say. She had noticed that he was wearing a shoulder holster—the breeze had opened his lapels several times as wind whipped around the vestibule. There was no gun in the holster. She thought he might be going to get it. No one would hear a shot this far back in a noisy train. That was her thought. He would not try to push her off, as she was strong and might survive a fall anyway.

Her next thought was to perhaps follow him back through the train but at a distance. But she waited too long. She imagined him returning through the baggage car and then the caboose. She panicked. She climbed the iron ladder to the roof of the caboose.

She crawled far enough along the top to be invisible from the vestibule below, staying on her stomach. It was windier than she expected, and the motion of the train back and forth on the track seemed far more severe than down in the cars. She held on with her arms spread out to find grips. She couldn't imagine what she must look like from behind, with her dress flagging open. Surely Antonia or Lowell would be along to save her. But maybe they would both get shot, leaving her to face the man alone, she worried. She closed her eyes so she wouldn't have to see any of it. Closing her eyes was something she was used to doing in her line of work. She opened them from time to time and could see the black smoke from the engine, curving far ahead along the track, though most of the time the little cupola blocked her view. She admitted that it was at least dramatic, and if things worked out, it would be a good story to tell. She worried that she was crazy to have reacted so. Maybe he was fetching a picture of his wife for her to see. She worried that there must be soot all over the roof that she was now reclining upon. She worried that the wind might be shredding her dress—she knew that trains could travel at speeds up to forty miles in an hour.

Davies stood before Antonia and Lowell.

"I wanted to show something to your friend, but I guess she went back to her compartment. I'd like you to share it with her and with yourselves."

He handed Lowell a letter-sized wanted poster.

"The man in the picture is Joe Willis, the man you have been looking for, I believe. I have a small suitcase full of these posters I'm taking to the police chief and the sheriff in Phoenix. I'm afraid the posters are badly made, but I had only an hour at a San Francisco print shop and with a poor sketch of the man."

"And who are you, then?" asked Antonia, "and how did you know we are looking for Willis"

"Miss, I am Robert Davies, and I am with the U.S. Treasury Department. It is our job to protect the president and, on occasion, former presidents."

"Do you have identification," Antonia asked.

He produced it.

Lowell was still skeptical: "You were seen with Willis in the lobby of the St. Francis, conversing for some time."

"For beginners, you are very good detectives," he answered. "I was charged with finding him and learning if he is involved in what we think may be an attempt on former president Roosevelt's life. I let him think I was someone I am not. In talking to him, I became convinced that he is not involved. But last evening, I received a wire from our Washington office to the effect that money has been traced to his account from suspicious foreign sources—Spanish— associated with this threat. Willis was in San

Francisco to meet with three Spanish men. I did not see the meeting, but we received information that it happened. The State Department has agreed to deport those men if we can round them up.

"When I got that wire, I tried to pick up Willis' trail again in the city. I returned to the cigar store that serves as a contact point for some of these men. The owner, who seems an innocent pawn in all this, told me of your visit, and he described you all quite well. I did not find you in that neighborhood, and I felt great urgency to get on a train in pursuit of Willis in Arizona. I was not and am not pursuing you. But why are you looking for him? I know you cannot be involved."

"You were also seen with the Taft people in the hotel, some weeks ago," Lowell said.

"Yes. I was there as security—I'm a Treasury man, as I said. President Taft was present, or about to be."

"Right. I understand now," Antonia said. "Here is our situation: We have reason to believe he ordered the killing of a woman in Arizona who may have overheard something a few days ago about the killing of President McKinley, ten years ago, of course. The victim, who was stabbed most viciously, was a saloon girl and a close friend of Miss Elsie Cork, whom you have met. I am Antonia Bonaventura, a deputy county coroner involved in the case, and Dr. Lowell, here, is a friend we have made along the way.

"In fact," Antonia interrupted herself, "please let me fetch Miss Cork so she can hear what you have to say." She stood and hurried from the car to their compartment. Finding it empty, she raced through the Pullman sleepers and through the kitchen and baggage cars and then through the caboose, as its door was flapping open in the wind and she'd always wanted to see one, anyway.

She paused on the train's rear vestibule for a moment to collect her thoughts and think of where Elsie could be. The wind and desert vista surrounded her in a way that momentarily took her breath away.

She glanced up at a snapping sound above her to see an embroidered blue ribbon streaming from the roof of the train. She recognized it as a part of Elsie's dress.

"Elsie!" she screamed, as she climbed the small iron ladder just enough to see more, though the speed of the train and the force of the wind kept her from going higher. Even so, she could see the billowing yardage of the dress sailing open, with Elsie's legs moving like the stigma of a flower, and her braids, having come unnested, whipping and thumping against the steel roof.

"Elsie Cork! What are you doing! You must come down from there or you'll be killed!"

There was no reaction, and she was certain that Elsie could not hear her. She descended the several steps and went instead up the safer steps inside the caboose to the cupola. Through its rear window, she could see Elsie hanging on in the wind. She slid open the small glass window and yelled to her. The wind carried her words and Elsie heard her and looked up, her cheeks smudged.

"Hang on, Miss Cork! I'll come pull you back to the ladder."

She returned to the frightening little ladder on the back vestibule and this time went as far up as possible, finally reaching Elsie's ankles and beginning to pull.

"Keep a grip, dear," Antonia screamed above the wind, "walk your hands back, or we'll both be blown off. Come back carefully and I will help your feet find the ladder here. We will get you down. Go slowly!"

In this way Elsie inched backward and finally onto the ladder, with Antonia staying also upon it and around her until together they reached the deck of the vestibule. Antonia hugged her and moved her into the safety of the caboose.

"I've ruined my dress," was all that Elsie first could say.

"It's fine," Antonia said as they both slapped the train grime from the front of it. It cleaned up well, thanks to the overnight rain that had cleaned the train. Antonia re-tied the loose ribbons that were part of the waist and bodice.

"What on earth?" Antonia finally asked.

"I thought that damn Abe Lincoln fellow was going to kill me. I'm rather sure he was. Where is he? We might both be in danger, Dr. Lowell, too!"

"We are not. The man is not a danger. Let's go clean up your face and your arms and I'll introduce you to him properly. He is quite fine. He is not the man we thought he was. Well, I mean he is, but we had him all wrong."

"I feel stupid, then. I've made a mess of things."

"On the contrary, dear, you have opened things up in a very good way with your forthright courage."

"Truly?"

"Truly. But this business on the roof will be our secret. We will say you had retired to our compartment."

"Wonderful. Thank you. You're very kind, as I would otherwise be quite the laughingstock."

"I am just glad that I was the one to find you, as you were putting on quite a show."

"I'm sure of it. They dance like that in Paris, you know. They show everything."

On their way forward, Antonia told Elsie what Davies had told them so far.

10. Rougher Riders

Percy Lowell, Antonia Bonaventura, Elsie Cork, and Robert Davies crowded into Lowell's spacious compartment, leaving the door open enough to avoid scandal. The lower beds were folded down to make salon couches.

"Dr. Lowell," Davies began when they were settled in, "you are in the best position to see if anyone lingers near the door. Do let me know, and please delay lighting that cigar, as I have been smoking these atrocious things as part of my work and I don't normally smoke at all. I am anxious to be finished with them."

Lowell tucked his cigar away and nodded for Davies to continue.

"Why didn't you identify yourself when you first saw us on the train?" Elsie demanded, crossing her arms.

"A fine question," he said. "I did not know your mission. It was only after watching the three of you and overhearing your conversations a bit that I concluded you were innocent citizens playing a dangerous game. That was my judgment. But it was in talking to you, Miss Cork, and rather at your own insistence, that I confirmed that fact."

Elsie tightened her arms. "I have never been called an innocent citizen, sir."

Davies missed the joke and continued: "You may know that this Willis fellow is sometimes called Buffalo Joe. He has mines and ranches throughout Arizona, and I'm sure you know that as well."

"We do, sir," Antonia said. "And we think, as you suspect, that he may be after Mr. Roosevelt now, having killed McKinley those years ago."

"Brava, Deputy Coroner Bonaventura, brava. But let me correct you about the McKinley assassination. Over these ten years, the Treasury Department has made quite a study of everything touching on that crime. We do believe Willis was sent by people still unknown to affect or encourage the assassination, but he was remarkably ineffective in recruiting help. He was in a Chicago jail for the two weeks surrounding the crime in Buffalo. A true anarchist beat him to it.

"Nevertheless, he returned to Arizona hinting that he had arranged it, hence his nickname. Some men believed his boast, including some railroad and banking men—a very small but very powerful group out of the District of Columbia, who were delighted that Taft was making their world safe again from the laws that Roosevelt had—excuse the expression—railroaded through Congress.

"Then, when Roosevelt became publicly angry with Taft's undoing of his reforms and began his campaign to unseat Taft at next year's convention, these men went looking for the man they believed had masterminded the death of McKinley and offered him three things: the first being a large sum of money, the second being their silence about his role in McKinley's death, and the third being the help of several men from Spain with the credentials to kill from an angry king. As far as we can now tell from a banking transaction, Willis agreed to it.

"We think the moment of risk is Roosevelt's dedication of the new dam that Arizona has named after him, as it will be in a remote location after a journey on a narrow, cliffside road.

"That is about all we know, or I know. I have a small suitcase full of posters—you have one—with a sketch of Willis on it, but I have no agents coming to help me soon enough, and I don't know what public officials can be trusted, as original plot, from those years ago, runs deeply."

Davies exhaled and sat back, having made his presentation.

"And so, the time is very short," he added. "The dedication will take place Saturday afternoon. This is already Thursday."

"Percy, is it possible to send a telegram from this train?" Antonia asked.

"Yes and no. Telegraph lines run all along the tracks, not to the train itself. But we can give a telegram to the conductor, and he will have it sent from the next station. What do you have in mind?"

"There is a saloon owner in Prescott we rather trust in this, Mike Wall—Elsie and I can both vouch for him as a solid fellow who would never have been a party to any political violence even ten years ago. He may be able to round up some men he trusts to get on the train when we stop in Prescott. If you want deputies, he can probably get some for you."

"Do it, please. As many good men as possible. We will use them to get the wanted posters up all over Phoenix. Brava again, Deputy Coroner. This is a very good idea. If we can get Willis held for investigation, that will put a shoe in their gear works."

"Sabotage," Elsie said.

"Beg your pardon?" Davies asked.

"Sabotage. The word comes from angry workers in Holland putting their wooden shoes, called sabots, into the gears of their factories."

"Well, that's good to know," Davies replied. He stared at her for a moment, smiled, then noticed her dress.

"You are a bit smudged, Miss Cork. I hope I did not cause you to hide somewhere dusty?"

"I was just getting some air," she replied. "On the roof of the caboose, if you must know."

Davies slapped his knee and then apologized again for the confusion.

"We have some time before Needles, the next stop," Lowell said. "And I'm quite certain we are not too early for service in the bar car if we might please move in that direction."

Antonia stayed behind to pencil-out the telegram.

As Lowell, Davies, and Elsie waited for service in the bar, Lowell noticed Davies' solicitousness toward Elsie.

"Miss Cork, I think you ought to disclose to Mr. Davies here your line of work."

She lowered her head slightly.

"The oldest," she said.

"Ah," Davies replied, "then I understand your fearlessness," and he patted her hand. "But the oldest profession is not in loving for compensation but killing for it, if you remember your Cain and Abel."

"Perhaps," Elsie replied, "but I don't think you're giving Eve her due."

The telegram to Mike Wall was sent from Needles, the last California stop, and the train moved on through the evening and the dark.

The party spent a short night in a trackside hotel in the town of Ash Fork, which still smelled of fresh paint everywhere and was mad with excitement because Teddy Roosevelt had just been through on his way to see the Grand Canyon and would be coming back the same way on his journey to Phoenix and the dam.

Antonia, Elsie, and their party then continued southward on the Santa Fe, Prescott and Phoenix Railway, arriving at the Prescott stop in late morning.

As they pulled into the station, they were hoping to see Mike Wall and any volunteers he might have secured.

"What on earth?" Davies said aloud.

Mike Wall stood on the platform of the Spanish-arched station, tipping his bowler to Antonia and Elsie, who slid open a club car window to shout a hello. To Wall's left stood six carpetbag-toting women of known reputation in their Sunday best. On Wall's right stood six more. He had emptied the rooms above the Palace.

"We're going to find that bastard for you, Antonia, excuse my French!" he shouted above the steam releases of the train. "We'll do it for Agnes Bailey."

The women with him shouted a whoop with waving fists.

During the hours downhill to Phoenix, the women were brought three at a time to seats at the rear of the club car for instructions.

Each was given a dozen or more of the Joseph "Buffalo Joe" Willis wanted posters and told to spread them all over Phoenix's bars. All were told to listen for any rumors of a plot against Teddy Roosevelt's life and to report them immediately to Mike Wall, who would be stationed at the bar of the Ford Hotel.

"If you're doing any business, you'll probably be at the Ford anyway," Wall told them. "But it's a nice place, so don't go in there dressed rough. Mind your necklines and hair and attitude, or they'll usher you out. What you're wearing now is fine."

One of the women, Bella Barnes, wanted the details:

"What are we up to, Elsie? Is this all about finding the man who killed Agnes?"

"That, yes, and saving Mr. Roosevelt from the same man," Elsie replied.

"You mean Teddy?"

"I do. It may be up to us."

"Well, then, we will do it," Bella Barnes replied and stood up in what seemed a warrior pose.

Davies asked Wall in a quiet moment if he hadn't brought the women instead of men because every wallet in the Territory would be in Phoenix over the next few days. Wall shook his head convincingly:

"Look, Davies, I get no part of what these women make. And, if you want intelligent, brave, curious helpers who can see through anyone and who can get into any group of men and go day and night and never lose a wink, just look at them. You wanted help and I brought you the posse, and I'm saying that word carefully. And, yes, they have all been itching to get to Phoenix for this shindig, anyway. There's not going to be ten dollars up in Prescott for a few days."

"You've been drinking," Davies replied.

"It's the air from my bar in Prescott," Wall said.

When the train pulled into Phoenix at sunset, Davies, Antonia, Elsie, Mike Wall, and Lowell headed to the Ford Hotel, where Dwight Heard promised to meet them, possibly bringing along Mayor Lloyd Christy and the chief of police.

"Dwight is here," Lowell said as they were still a half-block from the Ford Hotel. "That's his motorcar."

"It's beautiful," Elsie said as she slipped Mike Wall a peppermint.

"For a road machine to get you where you want to go, you cannot do better," Lowell raved. "That, my dear, is a Model Y Big Six from the Stevens-Duryea Company of Chicopee Falls, Massachusetts."

The red machine, its top folded down, seemed to take up half of Second Avenue. "It is what I covet in life," Lowell continued. "I love my wife, I love my assistant, Wrexie, I love my work and the miracle of the night sky, I love you all, but that machine, friends, is what this old man now lives to possess. I'd rather have it than a 100-inch Hooker."

"Explain," Elsie said.

"It is a telescope. It will be the world's largest. It is under construction in Paris for a California mountaintop."

"I should like to go to Paris someday. Wouldn't it be fun to go watch them make a telescope, Percy?"

The women of the Palace had already disappeared northward up Phoenix's Second Street, into the heart of the rowdy Deuce and its crowded bars and cheap hotels.

The Dedication of Roosevelt Dam was but a day away. The great man himself was due for the dedication the next morning by Santa Fe train, after a side trip to the Grand Canyon and a stop in Prescott to see, unannounced, the Rough Rider statue.

As Roosevelt and his family moved through Arizona, Phoenix was already in a state of complete excitement.

The town was festooned with banners flapping across every major street: *"Welcome Teddy! Welcome President Roosevelt! Welcome Colonel, Remember the Maine! Welcome to America's Next State!"*

Spring flowers had been planted in new gardens and boxes at every corner. Every storefront had been repainted, every window washed, every streetlamp polished to optical standards.

And every person of social rank—real or self-perceived—was still doing everything possible to have their motorcar in the formal motorcade to the dam, or to secure a seat in another.

11. Do You Have a Plan?

Dwight Heard—dark, tall, slightly stout, full but trimmed mustache, three-piece tailored suit—shouted when he saw Lowell enter the lobby. Introductions were made and the party of six retired to a side salon.

Davies handed Heard fourscore or more of the Willis posters. "These are for your chief of police," he said.

"He sends his regrets," Heard replied. "You can imagine how busy he must be. I have described your concerns to him, and he takes the danger seriously, wild though the story seems."

Heard motioned to a man who had followed them into the salon unintroduced. Heard handed him the posters and the man hurried off.

"He is the Police Chief's man," Heard explained.

"If an attempt is made on Roosevelt," Heard continued, "it could be anywhere on the way to the dam, there, or the way back. It could be in this very hotel, as he is having something of a reunion here with many of his Rough Riders before he leaves Phoenix."

"Lincoln was shot in the Ford Theater," Elsie interrupted. "This is the Ford Hotel. The nastiest villains care about such things. They want people to think they're deep thinkers and smart when they're pretty much three-year-olds."

"My god, you're right," Heard said. "I hadn't even thought about that. "How do you know the mind of villains so well, Miss?"

"We all have that in us," she answered.

"I suppose. And yes, he will speak here in this hotel. We can close off the affair to the public and I will suggest that they carefully do that. I don't want the event canceled, as he has several very important things to say. He received the Nobel Prize five years or so ago for settling that war between Russia and Japan, you know. Seeing Japan's thorough militarism up close has given him the idea that they will eventually challenge us for supremacy of the Pacific. He wants to get that idea out to his old comrades and see how they take it. I imagine if it plays well here, he will use it as an issue, if he gets the nomination again. He has also agreed to say something that I have written for him regarding how Arizonans might finish the job of getting our statehood."

"How so?" Lowell asked.

"Well, Percy," Heard explained, "I mean now that the dam is finished and our place as the economic power of the Southwest is well assured—and we have killed the idea that we should be joined with New Mexico—the one remaining problem is that Taft and several senators do not like the proposed Arizona constitution. We Arizonans have taken a great deal from LaFollette and his reformers in Wisconsin. That is to say, we've put many populist powers in the document so that citizens can put things on the ballot directly, recall corrupt judges, and the like. The plutocrats in Washington equate that with mob rule.

Taft is going to veto our statehood bill. That is well understood.

"Now, it is easy enough for us to take these things out of the proposed constitution, get our statehood, and then put them back in, but too many people here think that is unmanly. Theodore does not think so at all. He says we should take the controversial parts out, get our statehood, then change our constitution the way we want. I have asked him to say exactly that to the leaders here. They will take that as permission from the manliest of men, and we'll have statehood within the year."

"Will Roosevelt's help with statehood and the dam make you rich, sir, or richer?" Elsie asked—to the visible discomfort of Lowell and Antonia.

"I think those things will help every Arizonan, and yes, we couldn't possibly have gotten the dam as soon as we did except for Teddy gaining the White House. But, as Percy tells me you may be on the trail of unraveling the McKinley assassination, which investigation, by the way, we thought was pretty-well sewn-up, I will plead innocent. But you are right to think that people here might do such a thing. Water is the religion of the West, and Theodore Roosevelt is our Moses. But I want to assure you that Providence put him in the White House, not our impatience."

"I only asked if you might become richer, sir, so that you might afford a somewhat grander motorcar, as the one on the street seems only a half-mile long."

"Now, let's do talk about that!" Percival Lowell said with the excitement of youth that is regularly afforded the rich. "How long did yours take to be made? I'm going to order one as soon as I get back to Flagstaff—and just like yours if you don't mind."

"Not at all. And they will put it on a flatcar and get it to you within days of finishing it and testing it. You will never regret it, Percy. Driving it is on par with the first hours of matrimonial bliss. It will be my honor and pleasure to drive Mr. Roosevelt in a parade here and it to his speeches, though not to the dam, as I will be riding in the car behind him, and not in my own."

"Let us get to business," Davies insisted.

"Do you have a plan?" Heard asked. "Let me first tell you about something that will be in the morning newspaper here. A woman has been gravely injured on the Apache Trail, which is the very road we will take to the dam. It is quite a tragic situation, as she is the young wife of the dam's electrical lighting engineer. I bring it up because it a suspiciously odd thing to happen just now. Stage drivers are very careful on that road, and the stage driver was a man of long experience. I am told the woman is unlikely to survive."

"In my work," Davies said, "we don't believe in coincidence or accident until we are certain. What is known about it?"

"She was heading toward the dam in a horse-drawn stage that went over the cliff at a place called Fish Creek Hill. The driver survived but is in rough condition. He is being cared for in a stationhouse beside the road. It all seems a bad business," Heard said.

"Is there telephone or telegraphic service at that place?" Davies asked.

"No, sir—there is a line to the dam but I'm sure there is no line to such a small place as Fish Creek."

"How long, Mr. Heard, would it take us to get to Fish Creek Hill?" Davies asked.

"By horse-drawn it would take a full day, but four or five hours by automobile—all the way to the dam is about eighty miles from town, and Fish Creek is maybe sixty of it. I can't lend you my machine, as we need it here, as I said, but Maie, my wife, has a machine you may borrow—a Speedwell Torpedo that she will not allow in the parade because of a small dent and bit of torn steel in a rear fender that I'm sure you will not notice. Every other machine in the city is being cleaned and decorated for the events."

After continuously checking his pocket watch, Dwight Heard abandoned the idea that the police chief would join them; he suggested they remove to his home.

"You will all stay with Maie and me at our home tonight, and tomorrow morning I will show you the peculiarities of starting her machine," he said. "You will need to be on your way very early, as there won't be much time to do whatever it is you intend to do— Roosevelt will be here by 9:30 tomorrow morning and will leave promptly for the dam. He needs to be there by late afternoon."

"I think it's lovely that you gave your wife a motorcar," Elsie said to Heard.

"I wish it were so, miss, but the truth is that my wife gave both of us our motorcars. She is the money in our home—I married the boss's daughter. He is Chicago's hardware king, and she is his princess. I think I am about to impress them both when this valley blossoms from its ancient ruins."

It was reconfirmed that Mike Wall should stay at the Ford bar to receive any intelligence that might be forthcoming from the Palace women. He would then find a way to forward the information to the dam.

A bootblack was paid a few coins to turn the starter crank while Heard fiddled with the levers of throttle, choke and spark. An inaugural backfire briefly frightened the horses of several nearby wagons, gaining Heard the angry looks of their drivers.

"It can't be helped," he called to them. "Progress!"

As he slowly maneuvered the machine to the center of Washington Street and then onto Central, he narrated constantly: "They say some of next year's models will have electrical starters. I doubt that will do much for the noise—possibly make it worse, and another thing to go wrong, of course. Have you noticed all the smoke in the air? Well, let me tell you about it."

"I thought there must be a house fire," Lowell said.

"No, and you may find it amusing, Dr. Lowell. Mayor Christy, dealing through a women's committee organized an early spring cleaning of the city, admonished every property owner to clean up and paint their properties and tend their yards and gardens. These women got over two hundred dollars from me, by the way, for banners and what-have-you. Well, this call to beautify the city inspired a great frenzy of activity, but it did not stop with the yards and gardens. No, sir, this spring fever continued right inside the houses as people redecorated their homes, disposed of old furniture, and cleaned out their barns and carriage houses and basements, presumably in case Theodore Roosevelt himself might order a halt to the parade so that he could inspect a few basements. The great cleanup created huge piles of trash throughout the city. Well, sir, there are but eight men and two wagons collecting the trash for this city, and they were overwhelmed to say the least—and by that time, the great man was but a few days away.

"As you can imagine, this women's committee—these bloodsuckers, if I might say—came to Mayor Christy with a demand for action of some kind. He said to them, 'Ladies, you will be surprised what will burn if a match is introduced to it.' As a result of his comment, we had so many trash fires for a time that we needn't have lit the streetlights. The smoke still lingers, as it often does in this basin, but it will likely blow off before tomorrow morning when Teddy arrives. If not, I'm sure the women's committee will have us all out in our yards waving cookie sheets and Ouija boards or what-have-you to waft it off to New Mexico."

12. A Race of Men Making Canals

The short ride up Central to the Heard home was joyful for Elsie, who waved regally at the people who turned to see the elegant auto.

At one point Heard slowed to a stop and handed a quarter to an old man who limped out from a thatched booth where Central became a privately gated toll road.

"This is Cap Jeffries, friends," Heard announced to his passengers, as the old man tipped his tattered Union Army hat. "He fought with Meade at Chickamauga, isn't that so, Cap? That was a tough outcome for us, wasn't it, Cap?"

"We won the War, sir, we won the War. And unless you stop giving me grief for that battle, Mr. Heard, I shall double your toll, as I have threatened."

Maie Heard greeted the visitors as they entered a Spanish-style home built around a courtyard and called Casa Blanca. She lightly shook their hands with a demeanor that was less than warm.

"Maie, they will need rooms and will need to borrow your Torpedo. It can't be helped."

"If you say so, Dwight. You do remember that Teddy is coming here tomorrow with half the town? Where is my auto going, by the way?"

"They need to go to the dam, leaving at dawn."

"That is a hard road, Dwight; she really is a town car."

"It can't be helped. They are working to assure Teddy's safety. Mr. Davies, here, is a federal officer, and you know Dr. Lowell, of course. Miss Bonaventura is a police officer of sorts, and Miss Cork is traveling with her."

Nicely done. He will do well in politics. But she is such a school marm.

"If we destroy your auto, Maie, I shall provide you with a new one," Lowell said.

She smiled at that—the sardonic sort—and excused herself to attend to her staff.

Dwight Heard led them into a study where he pulled down a roll of maps.

"This one!" he said. "This is a print of Colonel McClintock's great map. Do you know McClintock, Dr. Lowell?"

"I know the name. He was a Rough Rider?"

"He was their captain. But more to this point, he did the surveying to determine the site of the dam. His topographic maps of the canyons are superb. This one doesn't show the road all the way from Phoenix, but I will give you those directions and you can't go wrong. But this map shows the canyon road—Apache Trail, as it is normally called, though for now it has been renamed the Roosevelt Road. It is in places a narrow cliff road that you traverse as you get closer to the dam. It winds up through the Superstition Mountains and was built mostly in '04 by Apache and Pima stoneworkers. They fit together the stones supporting the cliff roadway without mortar, rather like the Inca and Mayans, you know.

"Before '04, the road was a native foot trail going back to ancient times, so the route was well known.

"Here, right here," Heard continued as he tapped the map, "is that hellish spot at Fish Creek Hill—a steep grade ending in a sharp turn along a cliff, where that stage went off yesterday. There is a stone cabin there, a stationhouse, and that is where the injured man is being cared for until he can travel. Norton is his name."

Heard then described the route from Phoenix to where the route started on the map. Most of the roads out of town would be along canals.

"How do you already have all these canals, when the dam is so new?" Elsie asked.

"That is a very fine question. I wish we had an hour for me to tell you all about it but suffice it to say that these canals were built many centuries ago by a native race that created a great agricultural empire. We have dredged the old canals out and shall have another empire as a result. Our modern canals carry water from two rivers, but erratically. We have been suffering from floods and droughts for many years, and they have certainly been an impediment to statehood. Over the years, senators in Washington, sometimes to a man, have told me we are but a boomtown in a land of droughts. In fact, we get plenty of rain—too much to handle sometimes. We have just needed a place to keep our rain, and now we have it.

"By the way, if you come back during the summer, you will see that these canals and the countless open ditches they feed, and the tens of thousands of trees along them, cool the city on even our hottest days. We have built a desert oasis—or rather rebuilt it.

"I say rebuilt because we are standing on the shoulders of these ancients in so many ways. They were builders and farmers, artists and hydraulic engineers without peer, even by today's standards. Maie intends to build a museum to honor their culture. In fact, we have our eye on purchasing an ancient adobe ruin not far from downtown that will be preserved as proof that Phoenix is perhaps the nation's oldest river city. And you know, Phoenix gets its name from the mythical red bird that rises from its own ashes to live again, ever five-hundred years. Do you know how long ago the previous civilization has been in ashes here?"

"I suppose five-hundred years to the day," Elsie offered.

"Yes, give or take," Heard said.

"And five-hundred years from now?" she asked.

Heard paused and smiled at her.

"I suppose we are children playing at sandcastles on the shore," he said. "But it is serious play. The desert will be here when the calendar rolls around again like that, with or without another race of men to shape it to the needs of their families."

Robert Davies had not paid much attention to the lecture. He was examining the McClintock map—every cliff and turn along the road.

Maie Heard welcomes Roosevelt to Casa Blanca.
Dwight Heard is in the shadow to left.

13. In Casa Blanca

Three large bedrooms, each with two beds and a bathroom were assigned to the party. Overnight laundry service was provided.

Antonia and Elsie were soon in borrowed robes, having given their dresses over to a laundress. They were in a large bedroom decorated with the region's baskets, rugs, and ancient pottery, and were watching through curtains pulled back by beaded sashes as the courtyard below was set with linen and silver for perhaps a hundred guests expected after the dam dedication.

There was a knock at their door and Maie Heard entered, wearing lounging pants and a blouse of a bold oriental print. She had three small wine glasses in one hand and a bottle of port in the other.

She is what? Forty-two or three? I might please look like that entering a room when I'm older. Money helps. Lovely print. School marm face and bearing, though.

"I wanted to welcome you a bit more warmly to Casa Blanca than I did earlier. It has been insane getting ready. Theodore and his family will stop here after the dam dedication for two nights. We will have guests for dinner on both nights. After that, he will make a speech at the Ford and then depart. If that is not enough, Dwight volunteered me to help provide box lunches for everyone in the official part of the motorcade, about seventy people, which will be served at Mormon Flat, their halfway point. Most of the people hired to help me don't know a dessert fork from a spatula, but I think we are finally about ready."

She indicated with a wave of her bottled hand for three chairs to rise and assemble themselves around a small tea table with the guests' assistance.

"Do you happen to have a spare copy of your poster—the fellow you believe may be a danger to Theodore?"

Antonia produced one from her bag.

Maie looked it over and set it aside. "I will circulate it among the staff. But, as to the guests tomorrow, I think I know them all and none fit this description."

"Have you hired anyone to help that you don't know?" Antonia asked, "And will the box lunch for Mr. Roosevelt be identified in any way?"

"Poison! What a thought. Well, no, His will be the same, given out at random. Someone would have to poison the whole bunch of us. As to the help, there are some girls here from the Indian School who are new to me. They are trained by the school for domestic service, though some are a little new to food service. It is handy to have the school here in town, and many of us wives use them. They are harmless, I assure you."

"And paid little, I suppose. Where are their families?" Elsie asked.

"On the reservations, of course," Maie answered.

"That must be hard on young people. It is rather like an orphanage then, isn't it?"

"It is hard, I'm sure. But they will have careers and learn everything that other children learn in white schools."

"They will learn mostly to serve, I suppose. And could there not be schools on the reservations?" Elsie pressed.

"I expect there are schools of some kind out there. But I'm sure you're right that those families should have a choice. It is something that Dwight does care about. He is the model of the soft-hearted Progressive. I don't know who has the biggest heart for such things, Dwight, or Teddy.

"Dwight has a great deal of land in the south part of this valley, and he is subdividing it so that—now that we'll have reliable irrigation—he can provide it to poor families so they can do very well for themselves. I think it's a lovely thing for him to do. He also opposes the railroads and the banks, as a good Progressive, you know. He's for the workers, the little people, if you will. He is negotiating to buy the big newspaper here so that regular people have a voice. I would not be surprised if he is doing that just to improve Teddy's chances in the next election."

She paused for a sip and then continued: "Dwight thinks many of the big papers just represent big money, and they work to turn the workers against the very leaders who want to help them. It's often the young leaders against the old. Dwight and Teddy, for example, do aggravate my old father in Chicago and his business friends. But I knew what and whom I was marrying, and so did he."

"Your father may have enjoyed what Mr. Roosevelt did in the Philippine Islands, then?" Elsie said. "That was not very soft-hearted."

"I was in the San Francisco earthquake," interrupted Antonia. "Mr. Roosevelt moved heaven and earth for us—trainloads and boatloads and truckloads of all kinds of help. I still love him for that."

"Yes, that's exactly him," Maie replied. "But as for the rest, it's a hard world out there, Miss Cork, and I'm sure I don't have to tell you that. Dwight tells me you are a saloon girl in Prescott?"

"I am," Else answered with a smile, as if she had been asked about the presidency of the garden club. Their mutual stare lasted a few seconds too long for Antonia's comfort:

"Miss Cork has been vital to our efforts in regard to this possible danger to the former president," she said.

"I am aware of that. I do admire that. You are most welcome in our home, Miss Cork. My hesitation in the conversation just then was my own reluctance to ask a favor that may be too personal."

She then refilled the glasses, which had been evaporating quickly in the dry desert.

"I have often wished I could talk in confidence with a woman who knows men better than I do," she continued. "May I take this as an opportunity to do so? I can't possibly ask anyone I know."

"By all means," Elsie replied.

"I love my husband," Maie Heard began. "I love his big heart. He will do anything for a cause he believes in, and at any cost. When there was some talk in Washington of bringing Arizona and New Mexico into statehood as one state, he gathered fifty Arizona leaders and they took a train to Washington to talk to every senator under that dome to stop the idea, which they did. And he went another time with just a few others—one being the captain of the Rough Riders in Cuba—to change a bill in Congress to make the public funding of private dams possible, so long as the property owners paid it back, of course, and so that Teddy could then tell his Secretary of the Interior to send the first dam project our way, which he did. I expect Dwight and the boys had some fun celebrating on that trip.

"You see, he does travel a great deal and has great energy. It is my experience that leaders with great energy have more of it than can be contained in a marriage. What do you think of that idea, Miss Cork?"

"Yes, but I am sorry to tell you that it's true of most men, regardless of their position in society or politics."

A quiet settled in the room as Maie Heard stared vacantly at a particular native basket hanging on the wall between the canopied beds. She then turned her eyes to Elsie.

"Can you advise me on what they seek in their travels that might better be provided at home? I don't know what I'm asking."

"I do know what you're asking," Elsie said, taking a deep breath and smiling as a mother might smile at a daughter coming of age and asking the hard questions.

"Men are quite different animals from us. I'm sure you know that very well," Elsie began.

"I most surely do," Maie replied.

"And I think there are as many kinds of men as there are of women. But my first and main division of men is between those of strong character and those of weak. The strong can keep promises to themselves; the weak cannot. All men have a few lions inside them—lions that want this or that, women, wealth, other pleasures, fame, power. Some men are their own lion tamers in that circus within, and some simply are not. If there is not a good tamer in the ring, you're a fool to get in there with him. A weak man cannot protect you from himself. You might think you are strong enough to change him in that regard, but, Madam, the strong are no match for the weak."

Elsie stood and wandered near the window, but with a finger in the air to mean that she was not finished with the thought.

She masters the room with a finger. I must remember that and use that.

"Mrs. Heard, your husband clearly is one of the strong ones. You can see that by what he does in the world and how he takes care of himself and his family. But strong ones sometimes need to give themselves permission to be a little wild and pursue their own darkness. I am not defending them or my own work in the world. But they are complex creatures, and even the gentlest horse remembers when he was a stallion and from time to time needs the run of the meadow. When that happens, you don't need to break them again. You don't want a broken one, anyway."

"Well, I must say, I have not thought of Dwight as a horse, but I get your point," Maie said.

"It is the common thought that men on the prowl are searching to regain their lost youth," Elsie continued. "I don't think that is exactly true, but I do think they are searching for something they lost from youth. As boys, they thought of women as something magical, mysterious, and crazy. That is exactly what they are always searching for. What they find instead are women who are very real, less than divine, and full of instruction on how they should do their chores. When the mystery woman turns into their new mother, they must search anew for the mystery woman. It's rather that simple, I believe. It is almost a religious quest—the famous Grail Quest if you will, my favorite mythology, though it is hardly religious in its cruelty to the hearts of women. If it is a fresh young face he seeks, it is only because that is the age when he lost her. If he lives long enough and gets wise enough, he might figure out that that mystery girl is part of himself, and then he's got her and can stop looking for her in others. But that doesn't always happen,"

"You are well educated, Miss Cork," Maie interrupted.

"You have no idea—and at the University of Men," Elsie laughed, as did they all.

"Let me stop talking about men as horses. Let me talk about women as water. The water you can lead a man to. We are water, you know, we women. They thirst for us. We are the tides, the moon, the crazy dashing storms, the calm lake—ladies of the lake, giving men their swords—meaning their power and their reason for living. The ocean changes from calm to storm and calm again. It is crazy, deep, nourishing, fatal. The trick is to be the sea—including the crazy, so he can see in you the mysterious that his still-young mind seeks. But the crazy cannot be directed against him, but somehow *for* him."

"I wouldn't know how to do that," Maie said, taking a deep breath of resignation as if the teacher had gone too fast with the algebra.

"I don't want to get too personal, Mrs. Heard. I am your guest here."

"You are more than that, Elsie, you are being my friend in this matter. Get personal," Maie replied, refilling the glasses that were proving entirely too small for the occasion.

Antonia could see that the comment moved Elsie, who could not speak for a moment. Antonia offered to leave the room, though there was no place to go in a robe but the bathroom. Her hostess motioned for her to stay put.

"Excuse me for asking," Elsie began again, "but are you very proper with your husband in private—do you avoid doing things with him that you think a saloon girl might?"

"I am very conventional, I suppose."

"Well, you might think about that. But if you do try new things, insist to him that it's what you want to do and what you've always wanted to do–that every part of him is irresistible to you—crazy you—and you have resisted long enough."

"If I can do that without laughing."

"Yes. It's called acting," Elsie replied. "It's what we do. Look, men have it difficult in these modern times. They aren't the trappers and miners and cattlemen and gunslingers and soldiers that their fathers and grandfathers were. They worry that they are lesser men. They think they don't have the same kind of power. You need to give him back that power, you see. I know he is a powerful man in the community. Is he as powerful as your father in Chicago? Who knows? Anyway, no man is powerful enough in his own childlike imagination. Sex and power are as welded together in a man as sex and love in a woman. You must make him feel as powerful and ruthless as Genghis Kahn. In doing that, you actually have all the power. He is a Genghis Kahn marionette, and you have his strings. He will shorten his business trips to get home to his crazy girl from the village."

"And what about love?" Maie asked.

"Oh, that," Elsie answered. "Yes, the erotic can attract and maybe keep a man, but you wonder, does he really love me, or is this all a game and does he even know the real me?

"Well, here's what I think about that: If a man is full of his sexual juices, he is not really himself anyway until he has finally had a release, and then only for about fifteen minutes until he gradually starts becoming beholden to biology again. If he is warm and caring right after making love, then the real him loves the real you.

"In my world, right after, if a man is kind and lovely to me, that's the real him and I'm glad to meet him and serve him. But real love like we women tend to think of it—storybook love—is asking a lot from a man, at least after the first months of infatuation and flowers. After that, the best you can hope for is very much like what you hope for from a horse: They can be mighty useful over the years, can give you a nice ride every now and then, and you know they love you in their way. And for storybook love, read storybooks.

"Anyway, that's all I know. This port wine has made me talk too much."

"Thank you, Miss Cork. That was very thoughtful and immensely helpful."

"My pleasure. I do everything I can for the happiness of mankind. Believe me," Elsie said. "And by the way, the woman who served us downstairs—she is rather dark like me and is the sort who looks like she might live in a wagon somewhere on the edge of town. Tell me about her. She looked at me with such interesting eyes."

"Yes. She is very enigmatic and superstitious. She warns me about all sorts of things. She warned me that there would be danger in having Mr. Roosevelt here. I get so many warnings from her that I… well, I can't take them all seriously. Dwight thinks she is marvelous, though she is difficult."

"She is not pretty," Elsie said. "Her attraction is her crazy—her association with the secret world where a man's imagination wanders. She has mastered it. You might learn something from her eyes and her sense of mystery. I'm sure that's what is attractive to your husband—and not in an inappropriate way, of course."

"I will study her. Thank you," Maie said, "and thank you for your advice. It is wonderful advice, I'm sure—though perhaps there are some things I will leave to the women of your profession."

Elsie's feelings of respectability were pulled away in that moment as surely as if she were stripped bare on a street corner. Her face melted into a cold stare, which was returned.

Maie began to leave but fetched the poster and then paused in the doorway: "What time do you ladies want to be awakened?"

"A quarter to four, if you please," Antonia said.

"I'll see that your dresses are ready. You are both welcome to stay and let the men go do what they need to do to protect Teddy. I understand that Mr. Davies is trained for that sort of thing, and I expect you ladies might just be an additional concern for him."

"The thing is," Elsie replied first, "I need to do this. I lost a friend to this villain we are after, and I need to see this through. I need to go, and I'm sure Miss Bonaventura does, too, as it's her job."

"If you would like to invite someone to stay behind," Antonia offered, "you might consider Dr. Lowell."

"Percy?" Maie Heard laughed, "Heavens, he will dine on this story for years. You two are all he can talk about downstairs, and he wants to be a part of your adventure. I do understand that you need to continue on, but I wanted to make the offer. And, since you are going, I will ask you to help take care of my darling Torpedo, as men don't care. A replacement fender is on its way from the Speedwell company, so she will soon be as good as new."

Antonia said they certainly would.

"I feel like we're in a tomb, like an ancient Egyptian thing," Elsie said when they were alone. "All these treasures on display from a long-ago people. But the same people are setting the table downstairs and paid in pennies, I would bet."

She is more about justice than I am. Because she has seen more of life, I suppose. I have seen more of death.

"I want to tell you something about me right now, okay?" Elsie said after the lights were put out.

"Of course."

"I guess I don't want you to think too terribly of me. I'm not some old whore who is all spread-eagle on the bed when a man comes in and you say, 'Hi Cowboy, get to it,' you know? I talk to a fellow. I ask him about what's going on with him. I make him talk and I caress him, and I find the thing or two to love about him—to care about him. Everyone needs that, you know? My friend Agnes was like that, too.

"I know it is what it is, and it ain't pretty, but it isn't the same for every woman in the way she goes about it. For some reason I wanted you to know that. I'm sure Mrs. Heard doesn't get it. I've had some fellas coming to me for years and some have never had someone who could be soft with them and be a good listener and all, and I think I do them a lot of good."

"Thank you, Elsie. I do understand."

"Thanks."

The Apache Trail (the Roosevelt Road)

14. To the Dam

After breakfast in the grand dining room an hour before sunrise, the travelers prepared to leave for the dam. Antonia first made a telephone call to Mike Wall at the Ford Hotel, where a desk clerk found him asleep at the bar. It had been closed for many hours, but Wall had been keeping vigil as promised. Nothing had been reported to him yet by the Palace women. She gave Mike the dam's telephone number, which Heard had located for her.

Then, in the first turquoise light of the day, as a cool breeze rustled the palms above the entrance to Casa Blanca, they stood in admiration as Dwight produced the Speedwell Torpedo, a sleek, June-bug green touring car with a black canvas top but no side curtains. Fat canvas canteens and tin cups were in a box on the back floor.

Heard gave Davies a tour of the machine's controls and wished them luck as they pulled away with Davies at the wheel, Antonia in the front passenger seat, and Lowell and Elsie in the back.

They stopped half onto the street when Maie Heard called and ran out from the colonnade with a paper sack full of lunch sandwiches for their trip.

"I think we are to test for poison," Elsie said when they were at a distance.

There were no appreciable numbers of people on the street at that hour, except that they passed the

Central Avenue Dairy, where two men working atop a hay wagon called out, "Hey, old Abe Lincoln's driving Mrs. Heard's Torpedo!"

Minutes later they passed the Indian School and turned onto the side road of the Grand Canal. From there they dropped back down a city road for a few miles, then to the side road of the Arizona Canal, all the while in view of Phoenix's picturesque bare-rock little mountains.

Property owners along the way had erected posters of greeting to Roosevelt, whose motorcade would be on the same road later that morning.

The canals smelled of moisture and algae banks and were cool under the trees that lined them and drank from them. The desert beyond was in its spring wildflowers and blooming cacti as they passed the diversion dam. After a stop there to check radiator water and tires, they continued south on another canal road that would take them nearer the start of the Apache Trail.

But they were less than a mile out from the Granite Reef Diversion Dam when a front tire went suddenly flat.

"We have two good spares; I checked them just a bit ago," Davies said. He opened the toolbox on the rear of the Torpedo to fetch the jack and the lug wrench. It was empty but for a nest of old tire tubes.

"I'll go get us some help," Lowell said. "I need my walk anyway. I'll go back to the diversion thing. There were men and vehicles enough there to do something for us."

He strode off along the canal road, turning back once to wave and looking out of place in his wool suit. He wore a woman's straw gardening hat that had been squashed on the floor of the back seat.

"Roosevelt's train will be pulling into Phoenix in a few hours," Davies worried aloud. "This delay is not something we need."

"If something is truly afoot against Roosevelt," Antonia said, "the posters around town and our warnings to the police and marshals are already at work."

"True, but that is assuming Mike Wall and his girls didn't just dump the posters and go about their business," Davies said.

"He would not do that," Elsie offered.

"I hope that's the case," Davies said, "but I don't trust him. Yes, I will say that. I don't trust him at all."

"Why? Because he runs a bar? Because he knows the girls?" Elsie said.

The three remaining travelers were now lounging in the back of the Torpedo. The cool morning breeze was coming off the desert, waving the tops of mesquite bushes and bright-flowering ocotillo tips.

"He may not be exactly who you think he is," Davies said, almost reluctantly.

"How so?" Antonia asked.

"He is something of a mystery. There is no record of him in the 1900 Census, so he may have changed his name since then."

"The Census misses many people, many kinds," Elsie said. "I'll bet you a dollar you won't find my name."

"I would take that bet," Davies said, "and I'll further wager that he has never told either of you about his time in San Francisco."

"He has mentioned going there. Everyone goes there," Elsie said.

"In '06, days after the quake, he was one of the opportunists who set up shops illegally selling guns to the worried population. Over fifteen thousand guns were sold in that town in those weeks, and he probably accounted for a third of the sales. That's where he got the money to buy the Palace."

"Well, that's business," Elsie said. "How do you even know that?"

"Treasury was watching him, that's why."

"And why was Treasury watching him?" Antonia asked.

"He had a gun store in Tucson in 1900 and 1901. He was a dealer for Iver Johnson revolvers. When McKinley was shot in September of '01, that was an Iver Johnson revolver. Its serial number said it was originally sold somewhere in Arizona, so we looked at all the Arizona gun shops."

"It's a common gun," Antonia said.

"It is," Davies admitted. "But one of the oddest things about the whole affair was that the McKinley revolver was loaded with bullets that had insufficient powder. These were not factory bullets, but hand pressed, and with so little powder that they were essentially duds. Of the six bullets, five would hardly have penetrated skin. Only one bullet had a little more, and it was McKinley's luck that it was one of the two bullets fired. The other bounced off the breastbone, which is not much of a bone. It is quite a mystery why someone would hand a gun to someone for the purpose of assassinating a U.S. president and have it loaded with what the giver probably thought were all harmless duds."

"No theories?" Antonia asked, who seemed visibly disappointed and sad to hear a history of Mike Wall she had not heard directly from him. Her head was shaking a little but steadily.

"Well, whenever you have a big event like an assassination," Davies said, "you have what we call the *bright light effect*. It is just a way of saying that the immense scrutiny from government investigators and newspapers and everyone else after an event like that throws light in every dark corner of life, every illicit affair, every bit of political graft, every innocent mistake that now looks suspicious, and so on. If you put ten thousand dots on a piece of paper, you can connect some of them to make any picture you want. And so you can draw any conclusion, propose any conspiracy and have a supply of connected facts that make it look plausible. So, yes, there were theories. Many. I mean, everything in life is connected, but in ways we don't normally see. Just because you can connect random dots doesn't mean the connections are meaningful or occasions for blame.

"And to be sure, I had my own theories. It seemed to me that the person in charge of giving the gun to the assassin was not in favor of the plot but could not get out of it or blow the whistle. He thought he was saving the president's life, and he almost did."

"He or she," Elsie said.

"Quite," Davies agreed.

"Were you involved in the investigation?" Antonia asked.

"We are not supposed to say, one way or another. But if it answers your question, I will tell you that the serial number of the gun was A18915."

"And did Mike fit the bill in any way?" Antonia continued.

"He's interesting. He's not a simple man," Davies offered. "He's been in a few interesting places and has a lot of interesting friends in Arizona."

"That's just your bright light effect," Elsie said with some stiffness. "You really don't need to shine it on his dots or whatever. People think he runs the girls above the Palace and takes a percentage. That's Georgina and she is all right but not Mike. Mike is a square deal. He doesn't own those cribs; he just leases the part of the building that's the saloon. I guess we sell a bit of champagne for him, but that's it. He is the squarest deal in Prescott, as far as I'm concerned. And he would surely blow the police whistle on anyone who had the cowardly idea of shooting an unarmed man, especially the president of our own country. You'll see for yourself. If there is any way he can come through for us today, he will do it."

"I'm sure you're right," Davies said and then mentioned the lovely smell of the desert and checked the time again. Elsie remained visibly fuming until

Lowell could be seen riding high in the front seat of an approaching open truck, waving the straw hat.

The Torpedo was soon repaired and provided with tire tools purchased at an unreasonable price from the truck owner by Lowell, and they were again on their way, having lost less than an hour. But they were little more than thirty miles from their start, with more than fifty difficult miles to go.

The sun was getting high as they began the treacherous miles up the Apache Trail. Uniformed agents of the new U.S. Reclamation Service were stationed along the cliff road to manage the expected rush of automobiles, as any vehicle could easily break down and block passage. All horse-drawns were turned away. Any automobiles were required to have canteens of radiator water, sufficient fuel, and at least one spare tire. If there were to be breakdowns, it would be important that they occur after the former president had already passed.

Davies successfully showed his federal badge every few miles at these stops, sometimes earning salutes. He stopped the auto several times to compare the curves to the topographic map otherwise held by Antonia—he said he did not wish to miss the stone stationhouse and certainly did not want to encounter the fatal curve at speed.

"Why are you not married?" Elsie asked him as he rerolled the map after one of these pauses. "Or are you?"

"I am not. Lincoln freed the slaves, you know," he replied, getting a laugh from Lowell, whose dark suit best showed the dust of the journey.

"Are you related to Lincoln?" Elsie asked. "I mean…"

"No, not to my knowledge. But you know, I will never be able to wear a top hat or beard in this life."

By the time the four were gasping in unison at the steep and sharp turns of the narrow cliff road, Roosevelt's motorcade, far down in the valley, was just leaving town, making a first stop at the Indian School, where the school band played *Hail to the Chief* and the former president extemporized an encouraging speech to the students and their teachers. He praised the members of the several tribes who served with great valor in the war with Spain. After farewells, he gave a young Apache man the honor of turning the starter crank of the Kissel Kar, then shook his hand and took off his hat to him.

From there, the twenty-five-car motorcade followed the canal roads at high speed.

Close behind the motorcade were one-hundred and seventy-five unofficial vehicles from town, sending up clouds of dust that would soon be visible from the heights of the Apache Trail.

Davies and Antonia read the map carefully, slowing at a bend that revealed the Fish Creek station house ahead. Two automobiles were parked beside it, one with a medical cross and the words, "Saint Joseph's Hospital" on its door.

A nun greeted them at the door. Davies introduced himself as a federal police officer and then introduced the party in a general way as his associates.

"We should like to speak with Mr. Norton. As a good nurse, you will resist letting us do that, but we believe the safety of President Roosevelt requires us to do so.

The nun looked at him and his party suspiciously but relented.

"He is awake but please do not take long. He is inconsolable about the accident, so please go gently."

Norton was on his back in three casts; an intravenous drip was flowing into his available arm. Davies asked Elsie and Lowell to wait in the outer room. He and Antonia sat together beside the man.

"We are very sorry you were so injured," Antonia said.

He nodded and winced to do so. He stared at Davies.

"I thought for a moment, just a moment ago, that I got dead and you was Abe Lincoln come to fetch me."

"I do startle people with my looks, sometimes," Davies said. "But we do need a few answers if you will help us. I heard that this was not the first time you had driven a wagon or stage on this road," he said.

"No. Many times," he said in a whisper. "Many times."

There was silence as Davies and Antonia knew the next question but hesitated to ask it.

Through the window they could see the nun brushing the dust from Lowell, who stood chatting happily with his arms crucified in the air like a scarecrow.

"You were in a hurry, this time," Davies said.

He did not respond. He stared at the question.

"You had to take the risk," Antonia said, getting raised eyebrows and widened eyes that seemed to mean yes—you understand.

They let silence settle in again.

"Can you tell us why you felt the need to go quickly, even around dangerous curves you knew very well?" Antonia asked. "Was there some urgency that might help us understand any risk to Mr. Roosevelt, who will be coming in several hours?"

He slightly shook his head no. But then said,

"Ask Mr. Smith. I don't wish to do him any more harm. I have likely killed Elinore, his beautiful wife—at least they tell me she will die. I don't know what it is safe to tell you."

Antonia and Davies stood and were preparing to wish the man a speedy recovery when Elsie, who had come near the window from outside, motioned Antonia close:

"You should ask him why he was bringing the man's wife to the dam."

"I heard the lady's question," Norton rasped. He motioned them closer.

"I was not going fast at that spot at all," he said. "I stopped for a stalled motorcar. There was room to get around it, but just as we were passing, the operator of the machine crawled out from under it and accidentally startled my horses like a snake at their feet and we went over the edge. That's what happened."

"And why were you taking her to the dam? Was it just to be on hand for the ceremony with Mr. Roosevelt?" Antonia asked, touching a bare part of his arm.

"That's the question for her husband, ma'am. I was in a hurry for all that, but not when the accident happened. It's his business to tell more if he will."

Davies leaned in close to the man.

"I admire your discretion as a driver, but we are hoping to help assure the safety of Mr. Roosevelt. It is most important that you tell us whatever you can."

"I got an early morning telephone call from him. He said he was at the dam and to bring her quickly from Mesa and I attempted to do so. He sounded desperate is all I know. I left early with her as my only passenger to satisfy him, and he said he would pay quadruple, which is still my breakeven. He said it was life and death. I had her aboard within the hour. That is honestly all I know. I didn't tell that to anybody because a man's secrets are a man's secrets, but if Teddy is in trouble, you're welcome to that much."

When they were again underway, further climbing the Apache Trail, Davies shouted over the roar of the struggling engine to the back seat:

"Miss Cork, that was a very good question you had us ask him. Thank you."

It was noon when they reached the dam. They stopped at a wide observation point under a cliff. The great dam—the world's largest masonry dam, as they had been told—filled the view ahead.

"Amazing," Davies said. "You could have built an Egyptian pyramid with all those great stones."

The dam had been releasing water to the farms below and to keep the Salt River looking prosperous and the canals full, all to impress the great visitor, but great valves were now being closed so that water would flood out as if for the first time when Roosevelt pushed a button sometime that afternoon.

At the dam, a bee swarm of engineers and managers of all sorts—water delivery, power production, safety, greeting ceremony—were on duty for last-minute adjustments and rehearsals. Alvin Smith was the exception. A supervisor explained that the accident involving Smith's wife had sent him home to his cabin in Roosevelt, the small town growing on the shore of expanding Roosevelt Lake, replacing a smaller construction town, now half underwater.

Before driving from the dam to the shore of the lake, Antonia asked Lowell to stay in the dam's main office and attempt to reach Mike Wall in Phoenix in case he had any news to share.

In the tiny but bustling construction town of Roosevelt, Smith opened his door to Davies and was as alert and friendly as could be any man under the circumstances. His hair was neatly cut and combed above a young and naïve face. Somehow, he had dressed properly with a clean collar and tie, as if for a happy day. He invited all inside, where stools had to be improvised from packing crates around a small dinner table strewn with half-empty plates and an empty whiskey bottle. He apologized for all of it.

"The ladies here—especially the Apache ladies—have been trying to push food on me," he explained, carrying the plates away to a sink and then restlessly moving around the room, its rough windows open to breezes that were inappropriately pleasant.

How can this poor man survive this horror to his life? Do any of us really survive these horrors?

"Why do you want to see me? You look like some religious group, and I'm not in any mood for it right now. The nuns sent you from town, didn't they?"

"No, we are not that," Antonia said, "but we are awfully sad about the accident, sir."

"You may be even sadder if you like, as I have news that she will not survive this day," Smith replied, "and I cannot be with her. She is down in Phoenix and the road is blocked to all going in that direction until after the ceremony."

"We are terribly sad about it, for her and for you and for the life you were planning together," Antonia said.

Her words seemed almost more than he could bear. He swayed a bit and put a finger on the table for balance.

"Thank you, ma'am," he said, wiping an eye. "What, then? I don't mean to be rude. I'm not much for entertaining right now."

Antonia nodded to Davies to begin.

"We spoke with the stage driver, Mr. Norton," he said. "He is recovering but is distraught."

"Please tell me you are not from some law firm representing his little stage company."

"Not at all, sir," Davies assured him. "We are investigating a possible risk to Theodore Roosevelt at this afternoon's ceremony. Miss Bonaventura and I are public officials and Miss Cork, here, is our assistant."

Elsie straightened her dress at that.

"We need to know," Davies continued, "why you were in a desperate hurry to get your wife to the dam. You were willing to pay four times the rate, according to Norton. The explanation may be quite ordinary, but we do need to ask."

Smith stood silently for a moment, then found a small barrel that let him sit at the table.

"There are some stupid people in the world," he began.

"Amen to that," Elsie said.

"My job here was to light up the dam for the ceremony. That's all. I did that. It's all ready. The sky will be getting a little dark before the speeches are all finished, but the dam will light up beautifully, if there can be beauty in the world anymore.

"Anyway, these two fools knocked on my door Wednesday night. They threatened me. No, they threatened my wife. They said I had to do what they said. They thought I was the electrical engineer for the whole damn dam. Idiots. They said—and listen, I'm telling you all this because I'm a good American. I didn't agree in any way to cooperate with these goons."

Elsie spotted a half-full bottle of whiskey on a shelf and brought it over. She found some glasses and poured one for Alvin Smith. She poured one for herself and held it up in a toast: "To your wife," she said.

He stared at her and then clinked her glass with his. They drank in one gulp, and she refilled them. "You were saying?" she said.

"I was saying these fools said that when Roosevelt pushed the button to open the waters of the dam—and it's a ceremony, you know; I mean the water has been flowing and the electricity has been generating for nearly a year—but they figure when he pushes the button the big dam just somehow turns on for the first time, and all of a sudden there would be this big gush of water and electricity and they said that button should be wired wrong, and Roosevelt should get fried as crisp as a corn fritter. That's what they said, and they laughed. Kill everyone on the stand, if I wanted, they said. And they said if I can't make that happen, they would kill my wife. They said they had taken her from our house in Mesa."

"Dear God," Elsie said as she supported her chin on her fists at the table. "What did you do then? Did they already have her?"

"They said they did, but they had nabbed the poor woman who had just moved into our old house. I told them we didn't live there anymore and that was not my wife. They said they would find her if I didn't follow orders. Anyway, I explained that I was not the electrical engineer of the whole dam, but that I only did the lighting for the event. They asked if that included the speaking stand where Roosevelt would be, and where the button would be for Roosevelt to push, and I said yes, which was true, and they said I had better make that work for the purpose, or my wife, Elinore, would get it. So, I said I would do it, but of course, I didn't' mean it. I rushed up to the dam and used the telephone to call Ellie. We had just moved to a new house in Mesa, a few blocks from our old one. I did get her on the line, which had just been connected that day, and told her to get out of there that very minute. I couldn't think of where she could be safer than with me, so I told her to get to the stage—she was otherwise supposed to come later today. Then I called Norton, the liveryman, to arrange it.

"Describe the two men," Antonia said.

"One was a distinguished man, well dressed, with a Spanish accent—not Mexican but more Castilian Spanish. He is maybe in his mid-forties, graying mustache and hair, nice suit, no hat. The other is American, no accent. The Spanish fellow called him Joe a few times. He is quite stout, over six feet by a few inches, a well-nourished mustache, you might say, all salt and pepper, as they say. Balding but not bald—an older gent, but no gent, of course. Maybe fifty-five or so."

"That's Buffalo Joe," Antonia said. "—his nickname."

"I think you will not be safe from them, even now," Elsie said. They had a friend of mine killed."

"That's right," Davies agreed. "You should stay somewhere else for now. And I expect they will try something else against Mr. Roosevelt, since their strategy with you failed. Again, we are awfully sorry for your great loss. You should have reported all this, however."

"Wait a minute," Elsie interrupted: "You didn't do anything to the wiring that will hurt anyone, did you? Is there anything that needs to be undone?"

"No, of course not. And I thought the danger to Mr. Roosevelt had passed when God sacrificed my darling," Smith said. "But I feared arrest as an accomplice like old Dr. Mudd, I suppose," he added. "I got a ride down to Fish Creek Hill right after the accident, but they had already removed my wife to the hospital and told me I shouldn't go. Anyway, I visited poor Norton while I was there and told him to stay silent until I knew more."

"That was smart," Elsie said. "The police arrest first and investigate later, if at all."

"We have a baby girl, you know," Smith said. "She is staying with my in-laws. We put her there while we got the new house ready for her. She is okay. She's okay but she doesn't have a mommy now."

With that, he broke down into his hands and the visitors let him cry. Antonia put her arms around him.

Then they heard the roar of a flatbed truck coming near. It was Lowell, who had secured a ride down from the dam's office. He rushed in.

"I talked to Mike Wall in Phoenix by telephone," he said. "He has been trying to get his call through to the dam since shortly after Antonia called him this morning. The line has been solid with other calls. He has news."

15. At the Jefferson

Earlier that morning, the rising sun, three days shy of the vernal equinox, roared straight up Washington Street, illuminating the thousand U.S. flags and *Welcome Teddy* banners suspended everywhere along the eight blocks of the main downtown for the expected 9:30 arrival of the former president.

At the Ford Hotel bar, Mike Wall maintained his post, drinking lightly and conversing with a skillful young bartender that might work well for the Palace.

"She is calling your name," the bartender said.

Wall turned around to see that a doorman was holding back a woman who was trying to enter the hotel. She could see Wall at the bar and was shouting his name. She was wearing something between a robe and a sleeping gown—not proper dress for the hotel, especially on this day.

He rushed out to take her away from the doorman's grasp and talk to her on the sidewalk.

"Bella? What the hell?" he demanded.

"Two fellows in a room at the Jefferson. Me and Mary were entertaining them. I think they're Spaniards. They ain't talking Mexican the way I know it, anyway. But I could understand most of what they were saying to each other when Mary and me was taking good care of them. They said something went wrong with the big plan, but the new plan was even better. Then the other one said, like, yes, it will be a great thing—absolutely dynamite. He used *dinamita,* which is the same in any Spanish. Anyway, the other fella laughed so hard that I knew it was the kind of joke that ain't a joke. So, I says I don't feel well and I'm going to leave, and the bald one gave me this shiner and said I should finish him up or he would finish me up, but I wanted to get to you, so I made myself throw up in a corner of the room and he let me get out. He said something in English like, I had better send in another girl, or else things were going to be very hard on Mary. Anyways, I ran here, and sorry I didn't have time to dress proper."

"Wait here," Wall told her and ran back into the bar. He pulled from his watchpocket a large gold nugget that had been hammered into a worry stone.

"This is my lucky piece," he told the young bartender. I figure it's enough to get me out of any fix. Let's see if it works. I reckon you have a pistol of some kind under the register. I need to borrow it for a few minutes, and I'll leave lucky here with you for security. You could buy a case of pistols with it if I don't make it back."

The bartender stared at him for a moment. "I might like that Prescott job," he said.

"It's yours. It was yours anyway," Wall said.

The bartender slid a .32 revolver under a napkin. Wall moved it to the inside of his dress jacket.

"Careful, you've had a few," the bartender said.

On the sidewalk, Wall moved the gun to his pants pocket and put his coat on Bella Barnes. It worked well, as the coat was big and Bella small. They ran the three blocks to the Jefferson and took the stairs to the second-floor room. They could hear activity inside.

Wall whispered to Bella that she should knock and say she brought a friend, which she then did, and the door opened. Mary seemed to be passed out on the bed, or nearly so. Her head rose, and she gave a slight wave to Bella but then collapsed down again.

The two men were staring at Mike Wall, who pushed Bella back out to the hallway and closed the door.

He saw one of the men lurch toward his pile of clothes, no doubt to get a gun. Wall pulled the borrowed pistol from his pocket and shouted *alto*! The man froze.

"*Alto*. Kneel down!" he demanded of them both, hoping they understood. They did.

"Apologize to this lady," he said.

They looked behind, to Mary on the bed—and around the room as if they couldn't imagine he meant Mary.

"Apologize!" he cocked the pistol. "Apologize to Agnes here, I mean Mary." Agnes had been on his mind since the murder—she had asked him to walk with her to the Goldwaters store because she was afraid, and he had been too busy.

"Senorita…" one of them began, and they both made up some words of apology.

"That's enough. Tell me about the dynamite—the *dinamita*."

They shrugged as though they didn't even know the word.

"Mary, can you walk?"

"I think so, Mike."

"Bring me a pillow."

She did. He tucked it under his free arm.

"Look," he said to the men. "We know what you're up to. Roosevelt isn't even going to the dam today," he lied. "We have it all figured out. But you tell me everything you know, or you do not leave this room alive."

As the bald man laughed, Mike Wall folded the pillow over the pistol and shot the man in his head. The noise was loud but less so by the pillow. Smoking feathers and blood were all over the room. Mary was splattered.

He pointed the gun at the second man.

"Your turn to talk or die," Wall said.

"You're lucky you shot the one who only spoke Spanish," the man said in perfect English. "I don't know everything. We heard they will use explosives on the road, near the dam, where Roosevelt is expected to stop for a first look at the dam and for some photographs. That's all we know. We were supposed to kidnap someone, but she died in an accident. It was not our fault. We were not going to hurt her."

"Who is it? Who is at the dam?"

"A man called Willis—Joe Willis, and a man we know from Spain. The money is from rich Americans."

"All right. You get to live," Wall said. "You can get off your knees. Just sit on the floor. We have a few minutes to wait for the police. I'm going to tell them

I fired in self-defense, *comprende?* If you go along with that, I'll say you tried to stop him, *comprende?*"

Wall opened the door and asked Bella to come inside and translate, just to make sure the man understood the self-defense part. He did. Bella then went to fetch the police.

It took Wall two hours to get free of the police and another few to get through to the dam. He was not arrested but told to stay in town for a Monday inquest. That was a courtesy afforded the owner of the one Prescott bar known fondly by most Arizona lawmen, going back to Wyatt Earp and Doc Holliday, back in the day.

Roosevelt on the road to the dam; Dwight Heard behind him.

16. Dynamite

Lowell offered Smith his prayer and took an offering of whiskey from Elsie.

"Here is the thing," he reported: "Wall was at the Ford bar, as agreed, when one of the Palace women got to him, half-dressed and bruised."

"Who was it?" Elsie demanded.

"I'm sorry, I'm not sure I remember that. Is there a Bella?"

"Bella Barnes, yes. She is a tough lady—very tough, very fine," Elsie said.

"Anyway," Lowell continued, "Miss Barnes told Wall that she and another woman were entertaining two men at a nearby hotel, and the men were laughing about how the event at the dam should be *dynamite*. They were speaking formal Spanish, but this Bella evidently got enough of the lingo to understand that they were from Spain, and she figured they were using the word dynamite as a noun, not an adjective. She tried to break away from them and run to the Ford and report to Mr. Wall, but she was hit in the face and roughed up until she figured a way to slip out, which she did.

"Things got rougher when she brought Mr. Wall back to the room. One of the men died. The other one confessed at gunpoint that Buffalo Joe and a Spaniard are up here on the road, quite near the dam, and they intend to use dynamite to ambush Mr. Roosevelt.

"Why Spaniards?" Smith asked.

"We don't have time to talk," Antonia said, "but there are some people who don't want to see Teddy back in the White House, and these Spaniards are part of the plot—the King of Spain still holds a grudge against Mr. Roosevelt for freeing Cuba. It's something like that."

"I see it," Smith muttered.

"Is there dynamite stored anywhere on the dam site?" Davies asked of Smith. "If this is not their first plan, they are probably improvising, using what they can find in the area."

"Well, of course," Smith answered, "there used to be dynamite cases by the ton, when the dam was under construction—they made diversion tunnels and such. The remains of it are so old that it became too dangerous to move on these bumpy roads. Old dynamite, especially in the heat, begins to sweat-out the nitroglycerine in a delicate form. So, it was left in an earth-sheltered bunker here, and it will soon be underwater as the lake rises behind the dam. The water is almost there, I would guess. It will be no danger when under the water."

"Take us there, please," Antonia said.

"Whatever might help, I will do," Smith replied. "Whatever is too dangerous, let me do it for you," he added. "My life is over—the happy part.

The waterline and the remains of the construction town was but a few hundred yards from Smith's cabin in the new town on the higher shoreline.

"I expect the cases have not been turned in a year or more, so we need to be careful," Smith said. He explained that nitroglycerine weeping off the dynamite in the heat will pool at the bottom of a case, and sensitive crystals will form on the sticks. Turning the boxes upside down from time to time will keep such explosive pools and crystals from forming.

The dynamite bunker, half dug into the earth and sheltered with earth on three sides, had a rusted steel door standing open.

"This should not be open," Smith said. "Stand back." He stepped inside.

He came out to report that water was already a foot deep inside, but that two or more boxes were clearly missing.

"This stuff is bonded," he said. "It means there is a lock and seal on the door and a steel net over the boxes, sealed again by an inspector. All that is in tatters, and you can see where maybe two boxes are missing, going by the remaining shape of the net. A case of blasting caps seems also missing from a separate pile. Caps are mercury fulminate, you know, and even more delicate than weeping sticks. I would say any thief who thinks they can get very far down these bumpy roads won't get very far. They also broke into an area where things like rolls of wire and blasting plungers are kept. It's messy enough in there that I can't tell what's missing, if anything, but if they took dynamite and caps, they surely took wire and a plunger."

"Is it enough to do damage to the dam?" Davies asked.

"No," Smith replied. "The dam is like a new mountain, wedged upside down in a canyon. It would take all the dynamite in America to make it spring a leak."

"Did you see what kind of machine they were driving when they came to threaten you?" Antonia asked.

"It was a Lambert, I believe, a few years old, but a beautiful, black thing that should ride decently even over these roads. It has a frictionless drive, you know, the Lambert. It can climb like a billy goat. I still say it can't make it far with that load."

They returned to Smith's small house and looked over the topographical map that Heard had given them.

"Where, then?" Davies said, looking at it like a general.

"Well," Smith began, "there must be a hundred places on the road with cliffs over them, but you wouldn't want to go far with that load of touchy sticks, so I think there are two good places nearby. The first on is called Inspiration Point, of course, because it has a good view of the water side of the dam and is the final turn before you get to the dam itself. But it would take a truckload of dynamite to get that hill to come down, as it's a gentler slope. But over here, on the dry side, is Alchesay Canyon, where there's another overlook and the hill above it is just a funnel, if you will, for any mayhem above. That would be my pick, and I know for a fact that the motorcade will stop there for some photographs."

"That's just where we stopped to look," Elsie said.

"You could make quite an avalanche from right above there," Smith said, and they wouldn't stand a chance. If I were evil and set on such a thing, that would be my location."

"How would they—and we—get up there?" Antonia asked.

"Well, they've got a powerful Lambert. I don't know about yours. I would go a little way east on to this old mining road here. There are quarries up there where they got the stones to build the dam. That would be a rough road with dynamite aboard, but it would be possible if someone went carefully along. It would go up here, quite a ways indeed and steep, but only an hour or so by motorcar, to Deer Hill Tank, then cut back to Coyote Tank, marked here, then just overland to the top of that cliff. From there, they would work their way down on foot to all the outcroppings that could be blown. That's where I would do it."

Davies looked at Antonia and they understood.

"Dr. Lowell and Miss Cork," Antonia said, "This next part may be tough and dangerous, but I hope you will join us, as there may be places where we need your help pushing the Torpedo uphill."

"Of course," Elsie said; Lowell nodded his assent.

"Mr. Smith, I expect you need to go up to the dam and report all this," Antonia said, "…most especially the missing dynamite and our suspicions. The dynamite bunker needs to be secured, of course. You needn't mention the part about your conversation with the men and your wife, at least just yet."

"I will do so now," he replied.

The travelers had two pistols between them, and a jug of water borrowed from Smith. Davies said he wished they had rifles instead of pistols.

In the Speedwell Torpedo they roared up to the Globe Road, taking a faint mine road at the first bend.

"This first hill will be the toughest," Davies said as the machine slowed to a halt, but he did not let it stall. "Everybody out and push," he said, staying behind the wheel for the difficult work of gunning the engine and working the gears and clutch. Inch by inch, they made it to the first mesa.

After two more hours over the rough terrain, the party paused high above the Apache Trail to look down toward Phoenix and its wide valley.

"Take a look," Lowell said. "It will soon be lush green with citrus and fields, and I don't know what else—vegetables, I suppose."

"All Brussels sprouts if it's my luck," Elsie said.

Antonia spotted distant clouds of dust to the west.

"That must be the motorcade coming," she said.

Over the next rise, after a dirt cattle tank that they thought must be Coyote Tank on the map, they continued along a ridge until they spotted a black Lambert parked in the distance. The ground was all downhill now toward the vehicle, so Davies stopped the engine and coasted nearer and nearer and then stopped close behind the black machine. There was no sign of the two men.

The Lambert, and now the Torpedo, were on a steep incline near the cliff's edge. Rocks had been placed under its front wheels for security. Wood splinters on the Lambert's back seat seemed to mark where two boxes had ridden. On the front passenger seat was a box the size of an accordion with rope handles on its sides. It was pried-open and half-empty.

"Blasting caps," Davies said.

A detonation plunger was standing up on the floor of the back seat.

The party approached the cliff's edge and gained a view down to the Apache Trail. Halfway down was something of a shelfed outcropping where two men were working with shovels and fuse wire among the larger rocks—the ones that could easily be blasted to make an avalanche. Two rifles were leaning against a rock near the men.

Lowell pointed to a cloud of dust to the west, only several miles away and doubtless the approaching Roosevelt motorcade.

"Here comes Moses," Elsie Cork said.

"Look, we can't let this stand," Davies said. "They are likely planning to come back up here to use the detonator, but it's never smart to assume you have the upper hand. They might even have fuses—the kind you light. We can't let them finish setting the dynamite. I'll have to go confront them and disarm them. If I fail, send their auto over the cliff, as it may make a commotion to alert the guards along the road. Send it over, even if I'm down there."

"I have a pistol, too, Robert," Antonia said. "You flank them from the right. I'll go down from the left."

Davies paused to think. "All right, but give me a few minutes' head-start," he said. Antonia nodded, though she gave him only a few seconds.

I'll start down when you do. Wrong shoes.

Within five or so minutes, Elsie heard the men below shout to each other and she saw then go for their rifles. They had seen or heard something. Elsie took Lowell by his arm and pulled him away from the edge.

"How do we get their auto over the edge?" she demanded of Lowell.

"Are you sure?" he answered.

"We got two friends down there with little pistols, going after trained killers with rifles. You got to help me send it over."

She took the box of mercury fulminate blasting caps from the Lambert, pushed its nails closed, and used one of the rope handles to hang it from the Lambert's pronounced radiator cap.

She then sat behind the wheel.

"Percy, take the rocks away from the wheels."

He did so. The auto did not move.

'There is a hand brake somewhere on the floor," he told her.

She found it, squeezed its handle, and eased it away from its locked position—the auto still did not move.

"It's the gear lever then," Lowell said, pointing.

She struggled until it budged and began to roll.

"Jump, dear!" Lowell called, holding the door open for her and running beside the quickening auto.

She rolled out, into the dirt and rocks until Lowell stopped her and helped her up.

The Lambert seemed uninterested in going fully over the cliff. They pushed it from its rear bumper but to no effect. Its undercarriage was stuck amidship on the reef of the rocky cliff's edge.

"Lift it!" Lowell said.

"Lift it! We cannot lift an auto," Elsie called back.

"Yes, we can. The big engine is the heaviest part and is already over the edge. If we just lift the rear bumper… Trust me, this is science!"

As they did so, the rear of the auto began to rise of its own accord, and then so rapidly that it would have taken Elsie's hat, had she been wearing one.

The Lambert went over, rolling head-first with a Fourth of July display of small explosions and a spray of sparks. It landed upside down near the men who, cursing in two languages, scrambled out of its way and took positions with their rifles, using the Lambert now as a breastwork.

"Percy, how did that not blow up better?" Elsie asked.

"I don't know," he said.

She ran to Maie Heard's Speedwell Torpedo and found the hand brake and the gear lever and steered it to the same edge. She jumped almost a second too late, and, even then, the torn bit of steel on the rear fender caught the hem of her dress and pulled her almost under the wheels and almost over the cliff. She rolled over mightily and was free of the Torpedo, and she scrambled up from the cliff's edge with Lowell's assistance.

The Torpedo sailed effortlessly through the warm but dry Arizona air after one bounce on all four wheels and then hit the Lambert square, nose to nose. An explosion of several of the old dynamite sticks swept the cliff like a tornado, sending the two men below into unconsciousness.

By the time the four travelers reached them, one of the men—the one who fit the description of Buffalo Joe Willis—was near death and the other, though unconscious, did not seem to be seriously injured, other than having a smoking beard.

Elsie ran to Buffalo Joe and knelt over him. He was bleeding from lacerations in his neck and groin. One of the tire tools that Lowell had purchased was protruding from his side.

"You had my friend killed," she said, "and I guess now I killed you."

The man nodded as best he could and reached meekly for her hand. She let him take it.

"Mama," he said, "sorry, Mama. Tell Mike goodbye for me. Tell him I love him—and our sisters."

"Mike who?" Elsie asked.

"Your baby boy, Ma. Big fancy Palace Bar Mike. Tell him I love him. Tell him he was a good brother, and I was not."

Antonia noted the time of death at 3:35 pm.

The wrecked autos remained on the wide ledge, invisible from below. Security men from along the road and from the dam hurried up the cliff to put dirt on the burning parts and to remove the injured man to an ambulance, several of which were parked at the dam. Other men removed loose rocks that had fallen to the roadway.

Roosevelt's motorcade passed at precisely 4 pm, unaware of the drama but likely curious about the smoke rising from the ledge above them. The former president was in the front car, his teeth leading the dusty, bouncing parade.

Antonia and Wall climbed back up the cliff, and the four proceeded to the dam along a direct animal trail.

"I suppose you know, Miss Cork, that now I shall have to buy Mrs. Heard a new Torpedo," Lowell said to Elsie as they trudged down.

"There's only one way I might pay you back, Dr. Lowell," she replied, "and it would be a pleasure, but I expect your lady friend might take exception."

Theodore Roosevelt pushes the button
at Roosevelt Dam

17. Those Teeth

There then commenced endless speeches, seen but little heard by most visitors, who were packed in an L-shaped crowd along the top of the dam and one of its entry bridges. Theodore Roosevelt spoke with his waving fist to great cheers. This, he said, was the best monument a man could have. Elsie heard that part and thought it something a dying man might say. He finally thanked everyone again and then pushed the big button that, on the eve of spring, sent down more water from more broken rocks than Moses ever dared ask from God.

A married couple from Phoenix, owners of a small children's petting zoo, had brought a great blue heron that had been cruelly dyed red and improved with long red and yellow ribbons tied to its legs. The great bird was released from a small truck parked on the shore of the new lake. It flew first over the lake and then circled the dam twice before heading back toward the city, following along the water. People on the dam looked up and pointed, shouting that it was the Phoenix Bird itself, which was the impression intended. The bird survived the trip if not the embarrassment.

As Mrs. Heard's Torpedo was out of service, Antonia, Elsie, Davies and Lowell found seats in other vehicles for the return to Phoenix.

At the request of the former president, who immediately wanted all the details regarding the attempt on his life, Davies sat in that first auto, the grand Kissel Kar. Lowell rode with strangers in an auto he rather liked. Elsie and Antonia rode on the back dickey seat of a toolbox-laden Reo Roadster driven by the two mechanics who, in great clouds of dust from the twenty-some official autos ahead, had followed the motorcade up the mountain and now down.

They could have found better seats, but both women wanted to make a last visit to Mr. Smith in his small house on the lake's shore to again offer their condolences, and the two mechanics obliged them. It was a short visit, and they were soon in the dust at the rear of the returning motorcade. Smith had learned by message from friends at the dam that his wife had passed away.

The motorcade came to a stop at Fish Creek. Davies had mentioned to Roosevelt how the stage driver, Norton, had played a vital part in putting Davies and his crew on to the trail of the lighting engineer and how that information had combined for success with the word *dynamite* from the Palace women's efforts.

Roosevelt had stopped to visit Norton on his way to the dam.

"I am told Norton is not likely to make it," Roosevelt said to Davies. "Why don't we pay him another little visit so I can let him know his misfortune was not in vain. It might be a comfort."

Rough Rider veteran Wesley Hill was at the wheel and overheard the conversation.

"It's just like you to comfort a wounded man, Colonel. I'll start slowing down as we don't want the autos behind us to start skidding on Fish Creek Hill, you know."

Roosevelt and Davies went into the improvised bedroom of the little stone station to talk with Norton, who seemed weaker and paler than when they had seen him a half-day earlier.

"Norton, this is Theodore Roosevelt again," the former president introduced himself. "Do you remember that I was here earlier in the day?"

The man looked up and smiled.

"Two presidents!" Norton whispered, seeing Davies beside Roosevelt.

"Well, we just wanted to stop again and wish you the very best," Roosevelt said. "A speedy recovery is our prayer. And I want you to know that none of us can ever really know God's plan, can we? Your accident was certainly not your fault, but the effect of it—and your willingness to talk to Davies about it— was to help foil a plot against my life that may have taken many other lives as well, including the lives of my wife and son and other members of my family and leaders of this great next state. I know you'd still rather not be in that bed and not have gone over the side with Mrs. Smith, but there are great mysteries in this life and sometimes we must take them as they come. Are you with me on that?"

Norton just stared.

"Good man. Now, I want you to get some rest and some sleep. Will you do that for me?"

"Yes, Mr. Lincoln," Norton said.

From Fish Creek to Phoenix, the road was fast and dusty, with the little rear seat affording privacy that Elsie used to express opinions about Antonia's life:

"Mike's been after you from the minute you arrived in Prescott, you know," Elsie said. "And he's a good man. You should grab him. He's a sad sort, like you. You could cheer each other up. You lost your mom and your little girl… I don't think you can ever get over losing a child. I mean, you have to think they're happy up in Heaven if there is one, and that really is the Big Maybe, isn't it? But you can be happy. You will just have layers—an old sad layer underneath, but why not a new happy one up on top?... Mike's sad about something, too. I don't know what it is… Someone said he was married once, and they lost a child or whatever, and she was very ill for a long time after that, and he did everything he could do to get her the best doctors… Maybe that's why he became a gun dealer… That really doesn't sound like him otherwise… But she died anyway—nobody really knows and he sure as the dickens won't talk about it… I'd take him in a second, but he'd never marry a whore like me. He'd marry you, and you two would do all right. Maybe you'd let him fuck me on the side… Men need a little variety, or they go stale…I could have made my speech to Mrs. Heard a lot shorter, couldn't I? And, by the way, when's the last time you had a good cowboy—one who knows his way around a woman?"

"I'm not sad. I am basically joyful," Antonia managed to squeeze in. "And Mike has some things to answer for, especially if Buffalo Joe was his brother. Why would he not tell us that?"

"Shame, I expect. I'm an expert. He's a good man. And don't tell me you are joyful. I know that you're not in a joyful line of work as a coroner, but you are young and pretty and legitimate. You should laugh more than you do. There is a sadness in you. Whores know a lot about people, you know. We do a lot of work helping people get untangled. We are never paid enough for what we do."

Antonia hugged her shoulder in appreciation for all her hard work.

In Phoenix, the former president's car and several others turned into the Heard home, where Roosevelt would relax for two nights. The rest of the autos dispersed toward town. The two mechanics gave Elsie and Antonia transit to the Ford Hotel, where they were not able to secure a room. They had a few glasses of wine in the hotel bar, looking through the rush of people on the sidewalks outside until they spotted Wall standing alone and smoking a cigar. He said they were free to bunk in any of the four rooms he had secured for the twelve Palace women. They accepted. For himself, he had taken the room he had ruined, agreeing to have it redecorated after his departure.

Antonia did not ask him if Buffalo Joe was his brother. She decided there would be time for that later when he could talk long about it.

That was all of a Saturday. Sunday was for dining and drinking for the entire Prescott contingent, with the funding provided by Lowell. As Roosevelt was still in town, the restaurants were open in defiance of the Sunday law. Lowell was therefore able to get a dining room in one of the lesser hotels in a rougher section of the downtown—the only place not otherwise taken by the flood of Arizonans and politicians and Rough Rider veterans in their old uniforms.

Percy Lowell at one point looked Elsie up and down and commented that she had been quite rough on her dress. She laughed but was a little embarrassed by the comment. He saw that in her eyes and put his arm around her.

"Elsie, my friend, the Phoenix stores will all be open tomorrow morning. Goldwaters has a big store here. I want you to be at its front door at opening time. I will meet you there. I want all the ladies of the Palace to be there too. Mr. Wall's testimony at the inquest for that Spaniard he killed will be at 2 p.m. I think we should fill the visitors' seats with a very fine-looking group of ladies and all on their best behavior."

Elsie kissed him on the lips.

"Don't tell your mistress I did that," she said, "but you're always saving me, Percy."

The manager of the Goldwaters store was hesitant, but Lowell was presenting him with thirteen customers free to buy whatever they pleased, with the fortunes of the Lowell's of Lowell, Massachusetts footing the bill. The man seemed to know that it would be a morning of memorable pandemonium, but he relented, and shopping ensued.

At the inquest—decorated by the women of the Palace in the newest pastel dresses from New York—Davies and Antonia testified on Wall's behalf. Antonia described the connection between the murder of Agnes Bailey in Prescott and the presence in Arizona of the Spanish men. Davies testified that the attempt on Roosevelt's life was directly involved and that Mike Wall's actions in the Jefferson Hotel had certainly prevented a great national tragedy.

Elsie and Wall were alone for a few minutes in a hallway before the inquest. She asked him to sit down on a bench.

"Mike, you are a good explainer. You like to tell all the facts. I think I know something that could cause you some trouble. I think Agnes came down to you that morning and asked you to walk her over to Goldwater's store. She said she was going to ask you to do that. I want you to know something important: She wasn't going to ask you that because she was too worried. She had taken a liking to you and thought that would be a good excuse to have a little walk with you. That's the truth. You didn't turn down a frightened woman. If she was frightened, she would have taken the sidewalks, not the alley. The reason I'm bringing this up is that I'm afraid you'll get talking in there and you might bring that up. You might say maybe you were a little too anxious to protect Mary and the other girls because you thought maybe you hadn't protected Agnes. So, first, that's not what happened. Second, they will take that as a motive of some kind—like you were motivated to do harm, going in there. That will land you in jail or worse, Mike, so don't say anything like that. Stick to the fact that you were just defending yourself and Mary. And for Jesus sake, don't say that Buffalo Joe was your brother. That will send everything into a tizzy. Do you understand what I'm saying?"

Mike turned white to hear that she knew Joe was his brother, but he said he did understand what she was advising. The inquest panel absolved him and even gave him back the gun, which he returned to the Ford in exchange for his gold piece.

The killing of Joseph "Buffalo Joe" Willis took place in another county, whose officials recorded it as an explosives accident, as the interests of Arizona seemed best served if the entire thing did not happen. To become a state, Arizona needed to be civilized.

That Monday evening, Antonia, Lowell, Elsie, and the women of the Palace were waiting in the Phoenix station for the train to Prescott when six federal marshals ushered them into a baggage room.

Elsie didn't appreciate it. "We're not good enough to wait with the regular folks?" she said to the marshals.

"Just be patient for one minute," one of them replied. He had not finished his sentence when Theodore Roosevelt, Robert Davies, and two federal marshals entered the room from a side door. Dwight Heard was with them.

There was a hush in the room.

"Well, now," Roosevelt said to Davies, "so, this is your remarkable posse?"

"It is," Davies said.

"And Percy Lowell! I'll be damned. I heard you were involved in this dime novel adventure, and here you are! Ladies, I shall get to you in a moment, but Percy is a very old friend, indeed. You know, Percy, every time I go to the Harvard Club in Manhattan I ask where you might be. They last told me you were up on Mars to dig the canals yourself, just to be proven right!"

Lowell was more annoyed than amused by the joke.

"And here you are, making sure the canals of our own planet are full of water from this dam. Good for you. And you know, Percy, I am a canal man now myself, with this Panama dig doing so well. So, we must start a canal club of some sort. What do you say?"

Lowell didn't know what to say. He smiled and nodded, staring at the great teeth of the smiling Theodore Roosevelt.

"Now, let me address the ladies. I suppose you ladies know why my people think I should not thank you in public, and why some Arizona men think we should not say a word about the thing that didn't happen. They don't want Arizona to seem too wild and wooly just now, as they want statehood. But if you ladies had not done what you did, and if I and my family had been harmed, I expect the statehood thing would be put off for some time.

"So, though I can't make a big speech to honor you, I wanted to come here and thank you personally. I do have one more speech to make at City Hall before I get on my train, but I want you to know that I very well do know what you all did, and I will always remember it. Which one of you, by the way, is Bella Barnes?"

Bella meekly raised a hand.

"Let me see your eye," the ex-president said, "as I hear you got a shiner on my account." He put a hand on her temple.

"It's fine, sir. They go away."

"Well, you stepped right into the ring on my side, didn't you? I want you to know that I appreciate what you did. I don't know if I'll ever be back in the White House, but I'll at least be back at my home in Oyster Bay, on Long Island, in New York, and the name Bella Barnes will be registered with my butler there so that you will be welcome whenever you are in that part of the world. That is a serious and true offer."

Roosevelt looked over the other women.

"Let me extend that invitation to any of you, whenever you are in the New York City area. Just announce yourself as one of the female Rough Riders, for that's who you are—I hereby declare it. You will always be welcome. You do not need my address, as anyone in that state can give you directions to my home.

"Now, where is this Elsie Cork if I may? I am told to look for braids and dimples. You must all smile to help me find her dimples."

Antonia pushed Elsie forward.

"Ah, Miss Cork, I got the whole story on you from Robert, all the way down from the dam. You've had a rough go in life, but that's the West, isn't it? And I know what you have been up to the last several days on my behalf and on behalf of the memory of your late friend who was murdered.

"And Miss Cork, I'm certainly glad you've gotten to know Robert Davies. I've known him since his days in my White House. Let me say this to you both, Bob and Miss Cork: My chance of regaining the White House is slim, but whoever serves the people from that great residence would do well to have you, Miss Cork, on the protection job. Davies, see what you can do to get her into that line, or you'll be missing a good bet."

"Miss Bonaventura, here, has already sold me on that idea, Mr. President," Davies replied, "and I have arranged it so that Miss Cork will be returning to DC with me if she will but agree to it. It may cost the Treasury Department a few automobiles from time to time—her weapon of choice—but I agree she can be a great addition to our force."

"Bully. A new Treasury officer in the making. And now, if you all will excuse me, I must go give a little speech so you might have a better chance of winning statehood next year. Isn't that right, Dwight?"

Early in the evening, several hours after the departure of the regular train north carrying Antonia, Elsie, and the others, Roosevelt's special train finally left the station. The ex-president waved from the back platform as a torch-lit crowd of nearly every resident within a hundred miles cheered. More crowds would cheer him at each town along Arizona's tracks.

18. The Return

From Phoenix, Elsie Cork, Antonia Bonaventura, and their associates drank and ate copiously on the train. The women of the Palace filled the car like an Easter parade.

At the stop in Wickenburg, Lowell secured a case of champagne and sufficient ice to cool it. He had made the mistake of asking Wall what the women of the Palace liked to drink, and he had answered: "They are trained to ask for champagne, and they rather like it." So, a contingent of porters found a restaurant in Wickenburg with an extra case to sell after a cancelled wedding party.

The sparkling beverage facilitated the telling of stories from the big day.

"I want to know," Lowell asked Elsie, "how you thought so fast to roll those cars down the mountain."

"I'm sorry someone died, even though it was him, as I'm sure he was someone's son and someone's brother," Elsie answered, looking for a response but not getting it from Mike Wall.

"Mainly, I did it because I didn't want to see Mr. Davies and Miss Bonaventura go against rifles with pistols," she said. "And it was something of a chess move if you must know."

"How so?"

"It looked like something that could go on for too long, with Roosevelt's car getting close. Something of a stalemate might happen, with the great man in the crossfire, you know? I really thought the first car would tumble all the way to the road, and that would stop everything down there, and they would keep Teddy at a distance until they figured it out. It's called castling the king. That didn't work, so I sent in the second rook, if you will. It's not a famous move. Well, it is, I suppose."

"Is there a name for it?" Lowell said, sitting upright to hear the details.

"The move is called *kicking over the table*," she said, and Lowell slapped his knee and spilled his drink.

"You play chess, then?" he continued.

"A little. But it's mostly just in my bones and blood. My mother and father were both chess champions."

"Marvelous," he replied. "But with such parents, how did you…"

"How did I become what I became?" she finished his sentence. "If you will refill my glass, Dr. Lowell—darling Percy, and your own—I will tell you."

Davies interrupted as glasses were being filled:

"Miss Cork," he said, "you need not tell more than you'd like. Don't let the champagne…"

"No, Robert—may I call you Robert? I don't mind telling, and I'm not drunk—not yet.

"My mother was from a wealthy Boston family. One of her uncles was a great chess champion named Harry Pillsbury. He taught my mother chess, and he formed the opinion that she could become another great champion. As he didn't have the time or patience to teach her all she needed to know, he advised the family to send her to a great chess teacher on Joy Street, on Beacon Hill. She was seventeen.

"Well, she fell in love with the man, and he with her. He was from Jamaica. She became with child and was sent away to a convent to have it—to have me, you see. They placed me in a Boston orphanage, the Home for Little Wanderers, probably with a large donation attached.

"When I was thirteen and a half, I knew I was about to be sent away on the orphan train—which they still have going, by the way. They just dump children in the middle of the country where they get worked to death and otherwise abused, as I'm sure you can imagine—especially the girls. Anyway, before they shipped me out, I broke into the office and found the names of my parents. I escaped two separate times to go see each of them.

"I found and secretly followed my mother when she was walking with her ten-year-old twin boys. She sat on a bench in Boston Common and watched them on a playground. I just sat myself down beside her.

"I said, 'Hello, Mother! I'm your little girl,' and she just froze. The statue of George Washington nearby moved more than she did. I finally said I had just wanted to meet her, not to impose on her family. I knew it would ruin her marriage and her life if I imposed myself, and I didn't want to do that. She was my mom, after all. I just wanted someone to love, even at a distance.

"She just moved her hand to mine. 'I'm so sorry,' she said. She then turned to look at me. 'My, you're lovely,' she said. That made me feel good but also angry. It's hard to explain. I wanted to say, 'Of course, I'm lovely and how could you?' but I didn't. I just told her to think of me and pray for me and love me.

"'Can you come back tomorrow?' she asked me. 'I will bring you some money. I do want to help you. I think of you all the time and hope you are well.'

"Those words were really all I needed from her, and I couldn't go back the next day anyway, without being punished by the orphanage for my escape. So that was it. I have a mother. She's beautiful. She loves me. She was just a child, herself. She was in love. I love her."

"You will have much to tell her someday," Lowell said. "She will be immensely proud of you."

Elsie could not reply to that. She held in her emotion with a tight smile.

"And your father?" Antonia asked.

"He had died by then. His old neighbors on Joy Street told me that news, and they said where he was buried, which wasn't far. I took flowers that I picked from the Boston Public Garden to his grave. I had been thinking of changing my last name to his so I would have a feeling of family, but I didn't like it much and I didn't think it would do me any good.

"But right on his gravestone, balanced on top, was the cork of a wine bottle, probably from some of his friends who came to drink with him. So, I thought that might be a good name and I took it—the name, not the cork. I left it there. I wish I could have met him. He would have opened his door and just looked at me and known it was me without my even saying. He would invite me in and give me my own bedroom and we would play chess and read books and go for walks. We do that all the time in my imagination. He is quite a wonderful companion for me sometimes. I learned to play chess as a way of being with him, and I'm pretty good."

"He should have come and got you from the orphanage," Mike Wall said. It was the first time he had said much of anything, other than a complaint early in the train trip that the dam should have been named for Buckey O'Neill, not Roosevelt, as O'Neill was the one who set the obligation in place, and Roosevelt was just the traveling paymaster—a show horse, Wall called him.

"I can imagine that my father tried to find out where I was," Elsie continued, "and that my mother's family refused to tell him anything and perhaps threatened to have him lynched for rape. I'm sure he was heartbroken.

"I did get put on the orphan train and was resettled in Kansas City. I ran away from that family because the father mistook me for his wife —you know how that goes. Then I moved to Abilene and later followed a fellow to Prescott who said he'd marry me, but he never did—but really a sweet guy but just too weak to deal with his mother. I told Antonia about all that.

"So, I worked in a Prescott hotel restaurant—your favorite one, Antonia—until a customer recognized me from Abilene and told the owner I was a whore and not all white, so that was that.

"Anyway, you may not believe it, but I've had a good life so far. It's been tough, but good. I mean, look at the friends I've got—they fill up a train!"

A half dozen women from the Palace had been eavesdropping, coming nearer on the aisle as she spoke. They now gave her a whoop of agreement; "You have that right, sister!" one of them called out, accidentally spilling her own champagne all over Elsie and then laughing through a string of profanities.

Another of her cohort, with the assumed name of Lola, interrupted:

"Dr. Lowell if I might address you? The ladies have asked me to thank you for the champagne and biscuits and for everything you have done for Elsie and for justice for our late friend, Agnes."

"It was my pleasure," Lowell said.

"Yes. Speaking of that, you know, sir," Lola continued, "Sundays are particularly slow for us at the Palace. Men have their families and church and all that. Of course, we do spend those Sundays improving ourselves, reading Shakespeare and the like."

"I'm sure you do," he replied without irony.

"We would dearly love if you would come down to Prescott some Sunday and tell us all about your Mars."

"I appreciate your interest. And perhaps you could tell me all about Venus, and heavenly bodies more generally."

The joke was well received.

"Thank you, sir. You will find us very receptive and appreciative. I hope you will come. I hope you will enjoy our company so much that you will come many times."

Those traveling beyond Arizona, including Robert Davies and Elsie Cork—who would continue to Washington, D.C.—allowed for two days in Prescott for the funeral and burial of Agnes Bailey, whose body had been a week on ice at the Ruffner Mortuary, after having been given "the works" there, as ordered and paid for by Georgina, the madame of the rooms above the Palace. The dead girl's face was beautiful in the open-casket service at Sacred Heart Catholic Church. A red silk scarf was tied around her neck to remind the town of its brutality against women.

Lowell insisted that Davies and Elsie take a further day and night away from their eastward journey so they might see his Flagstaff telescope and something of the Universe.

On a quiet walk in a pine forest there, Elsie asked Robert Davies why, after more than a dozen years at Treasury and close ties to the former president, he was not the head of something.

"I look too much like old Abe to travel as any president's security. Such agents need to be invisible in the crowd," he said. "I was pretty badly wounded in a skirmish with bond counterfeiters in Philadelphia some years ago, and so have not been much use for anything but background investigations—though I don't limp as bad as I used to."

Elsie commented that she had not noticed a limp at all, though she did at one moment: when he was galloping toward the cliff with his pistol in hand.

Inside the observatory, they were silent as Wrexie moved the slow machinery so they might look at a particular galaxy of interest to Lowell. A complex scaffold of steps surrounded the telescope so that one might find a place to perch, regardless of the big tube's aim into the heavens.

"So many, many stars! What is it all for, do you think?" Lowell asked. "Whom do they serve?"

Davies thought the question was to him, but Lowell meant it for himself and so he answered:

"It is kind of a prayer, I think, to look at God's creation with studied appreciation. It is about truth. Seeking truth is the best way we honor His creation."

"The truth is a good prayer, yes," Davies said.

Lowell went on to say that a more powerful prayer was newly operating in California, on Mount Wilson.

"It is a 60-inch mirror if you can imagine that. A great dish on a mountaintop. The pieces of it, during construction, were nearly destroyed in San Francisco in the earthquake—I think God spared it in appreciation. I have not seen it yet, but I will soon go find it. I should like one just like it for this mountain, but not even my fortune will permit that. It took a great deal of Carnegie money for Mount Wilson—and now a 100-inch version is being built for the same observatory. Nevertheless, there is much discovery we can do here with this scope."

"This is your Grail Castle, isn't it, Percival?"

He stared at her. "You are awfully well educated, given your circumstances," he said.

Within a week, Lowell had ordered a fresh Torpedo for Maie Heard, and, for himself a blue Model Y Big Six from the Stevens-Duryea Company of Chicopee Falls, Massachusetts.

Antonia Bonaventura tried to settle back into Prescott life, but after a few months of Sam Dill's jealous contempt, she resigned for a position in the growing town of Los Angeles.

Mike Wall tried to get her to stay, even flashing a big diamond ring, but she decided she needed the ocean's sparkle more than just something on her finger, and she wanted to be closer to her father. She didn't like that Mike was still drinking too much and she didn't like that he had killed the unarmed Spaniard in Phoenix. She didn't like that he had not been square about Buffalo Joe being his brother, though she was sure he must have been embarrassed to do so. She even wondered about the gun used to shoot McKinley and if it had come from Mike, those fourteen years earlier.

She did love him anyway, and she knew it, but she decided that life with him would ultimately be tragic. The continuous show that was Los Angeles, with its growing movie industry and oil wells, its fifty-five-thousand automobiles, endless beaches and beach parties, and its murders and other calls for coroners, helped her to nearly forget him.

Dear Antonia,

Your old dad is delighted you will be living closer–an easy train trip away! I would be even more delighted if you would move all the way here to San Francisco, but I understand the appeal of a new city.

I tried to write a little poem to memorialize your brave role in the dedication of the great dam, but it's hard to write poetry about dams. I was looking for a way to use the dam as a metaphor for how we need to have a place for our rain, our rainy days, our tears, so they do not destroy us in floods but can be what we need to grow new life. But I'll just say it here instead: You and I need to move on with life and use the past to nurture us in flows that we can handle and not keep drowning in.

Is that a long way of saying that I am seeing someone? Possibly. Possibly her name is Lucia and is someone I work with at the dessert bakery. I would like such news from you, someday.

I did write a poem (enclosed) about how I think you have been such a blessing to your friend Elsie.

All my love,
Daddy

Grace is what we are given
When fortunes fail to nothing
For our sails are shaped to the gift of wind
And aren't the kind words of a loving friend
The breath of Heaven?

19. E Lucevan le Stelle

Arizona gained statehood on Valentine's Day, 1912, a year after the dam's dedication. It was a valentine paid for in blood—the Spanish American War accounting for most of it. Thus, a forty-eighth star was added to the U.S. flag—New Mexico having been admitted a month earlier.

Arizona women won the right to vote that same year.

Antonia traveled to Arizona for the statehood celebration. She went to Prescott, hoping to run into Mike Wall, but he had moved on.

Elsie made the trip from Washington, DC, and the two women shared a suite at the Hotel St. Michael. They attended the bunting-draped ceremony at the foot of the Rough Rider statue and stayed to visit in under the trees there. They were delighted to see Georgina, the madame above the Palace, up on the great porch above the bar, setting up her Victrola after the official ceremony below. She played an Edison opera recording, as she often did.

"What is it?" Elsie asked. "I've been going to operas, but I don't know a thing yet, really. Verdi or Puccini?"

"It's Puccini. From Tosca," Antonia replied. "I grew up listening to my father sing this as he shaved.

Then, if anyone was watching through the door, he would turn and die for us."

"Why is Georgina playing it? Why this one?"

Antonia thought for a few seconds.

"Oh, I see…" Antonia said. "It's her salute to the new American flag, with the Arizona star added. It's called 'And the stars shone.'"

"That's Caruso, isn't it? Can you translate the words?"

"Maybe roughly: And the stars were shining, and the earth was perfumed, and the gate of the garden creaked, and a footstep slid over the sand, and fragrant she entered and fell into my arms."

"She picked the right one for business, if there are any Italian men around town today," Elsie said. "What else do the words say?"

"All right. He sings: Sweet kisses and luxurious caresses; trembling I undress this beautiful body, remove these veils, but my dream of love has vanished, and I die in desperation. I die in desperation!"

With that, Antonia slumped down onto Elsie's lap and let a limp hand wither down.

She then sat upright as the music rose again:

"Never have I loved life so much! Loved life so much!" and then she died again.

The word brava came across Montezuma Street from the balcony, accompanied by Georgina's clapping. She waved to the two women, who then retired to the restaurant at the hotel for a long lunch. Their coats, wool scarves, and gloves, occasioned by the brisk morning, were taken at the door by Mrs.

Pelletier, the manager, who remembered Antonia from her regular breakfasts there. Antonia introduced Elsie as a visiting Treasury Department official. "You may remember her," Antonia said, "as I believe she worked here some years ago."

Mrs. Pelletier looked momentarily excited in trying to remember her, but then did so. Her smile turned steely sharp enough for kitchen use as she bowed slightly and showed the women to a table in the center of the dining room. It was nondescript, at least by Washington or Los Angeles standards. The doorways were arched in dark wood against bare beige walls trimmed at their tops by a wallpaper featuring draped garland. The lighting was by small electric chandeliers that may have been left over from the outfitting of closets and restrooms. The place was not crowded, as most Prescott notables had traveled to Phoenix for the larger ceremony, hosted by Governor Hunt.

"Not much of an event," Elsie complained, "but I'm glad I came. I stopped in Flagstaff to see Percy, as I think I told you I would. I was hoping he would come along to Prescott with me, but something was brewing in the heavens, and he had to stay. Anyway, I would have come just to see you."

"As would I," Antonia answered.

"I do wish Mr. Davies had come," Antonia added.

"Robert said he wanted to, but couldn't get away," Elsie said. "As fast as trains go these days, it still would cost him a week or so, and he couldn't work it out. He said you and I should be lauded as the heroes of the day, but that we never would be. He should include himself in that, of course, and Percy, but we can drink to ourselves, can't we? Let's order something here for that, which reminds me: After lunch, Antonia dear, I would like you to do me a great favor."

"Of course."

After lunch, Elsie insisted on paying with a hundred-dollar bill that sent Mrs. Pelletier running to the hotel front desk for change. The two women then went out front, then around the corner to the alley side of Montezuma Street. Elsie had asked Antonia to show her just where Agnes Bailey's body had been found. They went there and sat on rocks and were silent in memory for a quarter of an hour or so, surrounded by the last blackened leaves of winter and patches of snow along the quiet creek.

"I have another favor," Elsie asked. "Can we go see if there are any girls upstairs at the Palace? They might all be down in Phoenix, the younger ones anyway, for the doings down there, but I'd like to go up and see the older gals. I've been writing to a few of them from time to time, just to encourage them about how life has many chapters and not to give up. Anyway, will you go up there with me? You're a big hero to them, you know."

"No hero compared to you, I'm sure, and I'd be very honored," Antonia said.

They went up the alley stairs, avoiding the bar itself and its interior stairway that might give the impression they were available for business.

Georgina was the first to spot them.

"Well, the dynamite ladies in person, she said, and hugged Elsie and shook both of Antonia's hands. She called out down a hallway, and those who were not otherwise engaged joined them in the front parlor.

They visited for an hour, as some of the women and a few men moved through them on their way to and from the rooms.

News was shared, as the women of such places know more than the town's two newspaper reporters.

Bella Barnes was somewhere in New York City but had not written anyone in months.

Mike Wall had sold the bar and was in Chicago, but the word was that he was not happy there and was going to try Los Angeles.

Old Mr. McNary, the prospector, had passed away. That news saddened Antonia, who was planning to pay him a visit at the Pioneer Home that very afternoon. The good news about him, however, was that he died happy in a room just down the hall. Many of the ladies had attended his funeral, which they said was lovely—all pastels. He left a box of worthless stock certificates in spent mines to Georgina to pass out to the ladies, which were kept as treasures, as you never know.

There were questions about Elsie's life in Washington, working mostly in the White House. She told them that it was easier work than anything they were doing, and rarely as honest. She told them that Treasury liked its people to get law degrees, and that she had started on that, and it was easy.

Someone wanted to know how and where that could be done. She said she didn't know about

Arizona, but that she was taking night classes at a nice Catholic law school in Washington. The Irish women in the room gave a group *aah* of respect for that.

That afternoon Elsie and Antonia took a long, chilly walk around town to see what was new, then retired to a Chinese restaurant and then back to the hotel. They took the train together to Ash Fork the next morning and parted there with promises to write more often.

Later in that same year of 1912, Theodore Roosevelt was shot in the chest on his way to give a speech in Milwaukee. He would finish the hour-long speech before agreeing to go to the hospital, where the bullet was successfully removed.

From her station in the White House, where she sometimes played chess with the president, Elsie sent a telegram to Roosevelt, wishing him a speedy recovery.

For herself, Elsie traveled to New York City by train for the opening of every new opera, always making modest donations to the opera company in the name of Agnes Bailey. She annually sent holiday cards to Antonia, Mike Wall when she could find him, Mr. Davies, Percival Lowell, and several women of the Palace.

Elspeth Corcoran, also known as Elsie Cork, was admitted to the bar in Washington D.C. in 1915.

In the first days of that year, Mike Wall found himself living in the Boyle Heights section of Los Angeles, chasing gun contracts with the U.S. government and its allies.

By chance, he came across Antonia and a female friend at a restaurant on Main Street. The women invited him to sit at their table, which he was happy to do. When Wall was alone for a moment with Antonia's friend, she confided that Antonia had been having a hard time emotionally—had resigned her position with the county coroner's office and was thinking about completing her training to become a doctor.

"I don't know if she is strong enough—she has a difficult time concentrating and caring about things," the friend said, hushing up as Antonia returned to the table.

Both Antonia and Wall had telephones in their homes, and so they exchanged numbers. A month later, Wall called her with an invitation to lunch at that same restaurant.

Their first conversation was about the war in Europe, and that led them to talk of President Wilson, which led them to the White House and Elsie.

"I don't know anyone who writes longer letters. I don't get them from her very often, but when I do they take all evening to read," Wall said.

"I get them too," Antonia said. "Some are so beautiful that they really should be published someday."

"Yes. She is a philosopher and poet, isn't she? She writes about you, sometimes. I was sad to learn how you lost your mother and your little daughter in the '06 earthquake."

"Yes, I did."

"I am so terribly sorry," Wall said.

"Thank you. I just now expected you to make a little toast to them, but you're not drinking, are you?"

"Not much anymore. It's easier now that I'm out of the Palace. Anyway, I'm sure your memories are difficult, but I bring up your loss for a reason. I was in San Francisco last week for the funeral of an old school friend. His heart. Anyway, he was a fireman in that city, including in '06. There was a woman at the funeral, a Mrs. Coit, who spoke at his funeral beautifully. She is a big supporter of volunteer fire units in the city. I was talking with her at the cemetery, and I described how you had to say goodbye to your mother and daughter at the old Mechanics Pavilion.

"Mrs. Coit walked with me farther than she needed to, telling me of Gustavo Chavez, a firefighter she knows who took a bucket of ashes from the Pavilion before it was taken down because he knew many lives ended there. He took it to a Catholic church, and it is kept there under a marble side altar. From time to time, relatives arrive there for a small portion of the ashes, so that they might bury them somewhere of their choosing.

"Antonia, I know where the church is, and, if you are interested, I will take you and your father there, at your convenience. Ms. Coit suggested that Pioneer Park on Telegraph Hill is a place where many people distribute ashes—nice views of the city and the bay, of course."

Wall did not expect that Antonia would cry, but she did, and so copiously that he took her a few steps up a stairway and held her until she regained her composure.

The journey he suggested was accomplished several months later. In a sunrise ceremony, Tony Bonaventura had words of love for his wife and granddaughter as his daughter commended their ashes to the earth of Telegraph Hill:

> "Oh, Darlings! This sprinkling of your spirit makes this lovely hill so much higher now! Please watch down on us from this Heaven, as we look ever up to you in love!"

The grand view from the hill could not but remind Antonia of how beautiful the city had also been on a morning nine years earlier—until the first seconds of the quake. It had become like the cities of Europe, built upon the ruins of former worlds.

And for now, broken clouds of sea fog moved swiftly overhead, sweeping the city with spotlights of rising sunshine, and making the artfully populated hills of the city seem to undulate and sparkle as if the whole peninsula were alive and breathing. *It could happen again, any second—whatever is beneath could shake us off again,* she thought, though it did not diminish her smile.

How brave we all are, was her thought, *that we make our lives of love, and we strive for joy, though from wreckage we have come and to wreckage we will return.* It did not bother her that the ashes of her mother and her child were uncertainly in the mix with the plaster and cement and carbon of the great quake and fire—in fact, it was somehow a comfort that, in the grand view of Creation as embraced by Percy and his Mojave elder visitors, everything and everyone was an undivided part of the Great Thing.

On the train back to Los Angeles, Wall was quiet until Antonia told him to go ahead and say it, whatever it was.

"It's you," he said.

"First, I sincerely want to encourage you to become a doctor. You could stay at your father's house and study nearby. You've been in the death business since '06, and I think It's time you got on the other side of the line—to live again among the living."

She nodded.

"I really do appreciate your…" she began, but he interrupted:

"Elsie wrote me recently after corresponding with you. She told me to give you a boost toward the medical school thing. I wish I could say I was that thoughtful."

"You're plenty thoughtful," she said. "This trip— the ashes. I'm not going to cry, but really, Mike."

"Anyway, Antonia, Los Angeles has a good medical school, too. There's something I want to say about that."

Antonia could see that he was hesitating and slightly blushing.

"Are you going to suggest that I could stay with you, Mike?"

"I guess I am. I mean, there's an extra room that nobody's using. Hate to see it go to waste. Wouldn't mind the company."

"And we would what—say I'm your sister?"

"Look… you see, Antonia… I'm, I'm…"

"Hopeless," she said. "Why don't you tell me what you're feeling?"

"I think about you all the time," he said. "I still do think about my Betsy and the old days, but it's getting so that I don't feel like half a human anymore—at least not all the time. I mean, half of me was her—the better half, like they say. I've tried to not feel sorry for myself. My loss was nothing compared to my wife's—to lose everything, the birds, the joys all around us—to look up at the sky and say 'nice.' The love. All the love. It is her loss of those things that has made me sad for so long. That I was not able to save her from that loss—and the child, too.

"Elsie told me in a letter once—it was mostly about losing my brother—that grieving is hard because it rips off the blindfold and we see mortality itself. We go through daily life as if in a trance, but then something like this happens and we see the truth of our situation. We are all on the hangman's scaffold, you see. We forget we are there. We can dance and sing up there because we forget our situation, hypnotized.

"Anyway," Wall continued, "I need to forget again and be able to dance up there, you know? Dance with someone. And these days, well, I think about you so often and wonder how you are doing and what I might do for you—you know—if anything—if you'd want anything. I want to be helpful. I want to look after you."

"I look after myself. I have enough savings to go to medical school and pay for my house, too."

"I know. I know. But it's what I need. It's who I need to be. You have a great spirit, Antonia, and I feel a lot better—a lot more alive, really—not half alive—when I'm around you or even thinking about you. I want you to never fear anything, is what I'm saying. I want you to know that someone has your back and your hand—on days when you might want that, of course. I want to be there so that nothing can ever harm you.

"You know the way you and old Percy sort of saved Elsie from her past? I think someone needs to do that for you, Antonia, and I think I'm the one for it."

"Do you suppose there's a word for that feeling you're having, Mike?"

He seemed genuinely confused by the question, so she couldn't suppress a small laugh.

"Don't laugh at this poor old son-of-a-bitch, Antonia. I know the word you mean. Do you want me to say the word?"

"Let me think about that," she replied, patting his hand. "I think I started really breathing again up on Telegraph Hill for the first time in a very long time. Let me get used to breathing for a little while and then let's figure it out."

"Okay, girl. Mind if I call you girl?"

"That's fine, Mike," she said and patted his hand again.

"Why didn't you ever tell us that Buffalo Joe was your brother? And what about that gun that killed

McKinley?" She had wanted to ask him the questions to his face for these four years.

"Joe was crazy," he said. "I loved him, but he was crazy. He bankrolled me several times before I got the hang of business. He never carried a gun because he knew he was crazy and had an anger problem. I certainly never gave him a gun. I had no idea he was mixed up with the McKinley thing if he even was. Anyway, like Davies said, Joe was picked up and was in jail during all of that. Anyway, I didn't tell you he was my brother because I was in love with you, even back when we first met, Antonia, and you would have sent me packing. That's why. I'm sorry."

"Just wanted to know," she said, and patted his hand once again and then squeezed it.

Mrs. Heard's new Speedwell Torpedo

Epilogue

April 15, 1915

Dear Antonia,

What a joy to hear about you and Mike! I tried very hard to attend, as I'm sure you must know. The troubles in Europe have made Mr. Wilson's White House busier than usual, and it is always busy enough, anyway. I'm sure you got my regrets, but I want you to know more fully that I tried and that I deeply regret not being there. You have both meant everything to my life! In my defense, your marriage did seem a bit rushed, and I should like to guess a good reason for that!

I'm happy to hear that Robert was able to be there. His section of Treasury is a little calmer than the Secret Service part, and we in the Secret Service are mostly a younger bunch—quicker on our feet— though I wouldn't mention that to him if I were you.

He could have headed up the Secret Service after Arizona, as he was such a hero, but I think what he wanted out of that success was just a redemption of a sort after being in the Service when McKinley was killed, though Robert wasn't in charge of that disaster in any way. But he took it so personally. Now, as he may have told you if you've had time to chat, he's in charge of arresting counterfeiters in all 48 states and he says he enjoys it. Maybe he'll bring us some of the better stuff someday—he should have brought you some as a wedding present!

I have an idea. I'll print up some fake money and hope he arrests me! He's been too busy for me otherwise! I'll put my picture on the bills instead of Washington and Lincoln, so he knows whom to come get.

Some time ago you asked me for more of my story. I promise to come see you and Mike as soon as I can and we'll go on a long picnic and talk and talk.

But I'll give you one story now, because it fits what I want to say to you and because of what you wrote about Mike talking about the need to share beauty.

So, when Agnes and I were sent with maybe 100 other children from Boston to Kansas City on the orphan train, there was a strange occurrence. We pulled into a small-town station somewhere in southern Missouri and suddenly all the townspeople were standing on the platform with their mouths open. A couple of preachers were preaching. Somewhere behind us, there was a railroad bridge that had washed out. People in the previous station saw us barrel right past the warning barricades and disappear into the woods. They figured we must have gone over into a river. But we arrived in this little town on the other side, just as the town was getting ready to go recover bodies—having got the wire from the other station. The train engineer swore he didn't see any barricades or any bridge out. He went back to the bridge by a motorcar and, sure enough, it was completely out. He came back shaking his head and we kept going.

All of us young people were so quiet after that. It was dark. Agnes took my arm and got right into my face so we could see each other through the gloom. She wondered if maybe we had all been killed and now were going to Heaven.

If I could talk to her now, I would know to say, yes, this whole thing is surely a miracle and we are Heaven-bound, or something like it, and everyone is on an orphan train of a sort. And, for myself, I thought, if it happened to be a miracle and not some story told to us by the conductor—who did tell us stories, and who did comment that we were in God's hands and heading to good lives—that it meant that I was meant to do something special with my life, and that thought has sustained me through many difficult times.

But surely life and its miracles aren't worth all the suffering unless shared. And that's what gives me such joy for you and Mike, and you can bet (he can bet—he always does) that Robert and I won't be far behind you. The man does not stand a chance.

Thank you for your friendship, Antonia. You have been in my life "the breath of Heaven"—to quote from your father's poem, which I have embroidered.

All my Love,
Elsie

P.S. I finally saw Birth of a Nation. Your wire of warning was so right. It is atrocious. The worst part was the audience.

May 1, 1915

My Dearest Dear Friend, Elsie,
I can't thank you enough for your beautiful letter and your good wishes for us. I know it was impossible for you, with your responsibilities there, but I do wish you could have been at the ceremony, particularly for the moment when the priest asked Mike if he would take me as his wedded wife, etcetera, etcetera. The poor man froze. His eyes locked into mine and he absolutely could not think of what he was supposed to say. I asked him, "Mike, do you love me?" He immediately responded, "I do!" and that was good enough for the priest!

And, yes, it was great that Robert was there, and so was Percy and Mrs. Lowell (not Wrexie!). He said he is holding back on a wedding present because he wants to wait and give a fine telescope to our first child—but there was a bank draft slipped to Mike, anyway!

We are just now about to depart on what I will call a honeymoon, though we are taking my darling father with us, which may seem odd for a honeymoon. But it is a chance for him to see Sicily, the land of his youth, and it will be lovely to see it with him. I'll start medical school at the University of Southern California when we return. It's a Methodist college, but medicine is medicine.

We are on a magnificent ship, ensconced in the loveliest of staterooms. I will write to you more fully when we are at sea and I have time for a long one, which you deserve, as I have been remiss in writing you lately. I am just jotting off this short note so that I can have it posted before we "shove off."

Mike has promised me that he will get out of the gun business, and he says this trip is the end of it and will set him up royally (his word) for whatever he might do next. I suppose I can't complain too much, as his dealings are paying for this trip, as least as far as Liverpool. From there we will see some of England and then cross the Channel to see the south of France—then by train to Naples and then to Sicily on a sailboat that will stop in lovely places along the way, particularly Sorrento and the towns of the Amalfi Coast, which are supposed to be gorgeous. Don't worry, we are going through places that are not in conflict.

I was very happy to hear that Robert is doing so well at Treasury, and happy that you get to see him from time to time. I hope that you can make that even more frequent, as he is as good a man as anyone will ever find, and I know he loves you dearly.

As you said in your wonderful letter, the beauty of life requires sharing. It is so short, after all, so short that I sometimes think that God is a child blowing pretty bubbles and we are them. It goes fast, and we must make every day and every night count as an opportunity for love.

Your friend,
Antonia

On May 8, 1915, Elsie Cork received from Dublin, Ireland the following telegram at the White House: ELSIE DEAR YOU HEARD ABOUT THE LUSITANIA. IT WAS HORRIBLE. LONG LETTER TO FOLLOW. OUR FAMILY OK. YES ALL FOUR. BUT MANY TRAGICALLY LOST INCLUDING NEW FRIENDS WE JUST MET.

May 27, 1917

Dear Elsie,

I have been in touch with Robert Davies in the hope that he might tell me you are all right and give me a proper address for you. He was quite adamant in saying he cannot tell me what you are up to "over there," and says he has not been able to contact you himself, though he suggested a letter addressed to you at the U.S. Embassy in London might find you at some point.

I have some other news: When that German telegram was intercepted and filled our newspaper headlines here—the Zimmerman one where Germany promised Mexico might have back Arizona and a few other states if Mexico would join the war against us, all you-know-what broke loose in Arizona and I guess everywhere else, too. Two months later we were at war, of course.

Mike's Arizona friends wanted him to provide arms for some kind of latter-day Rough Rider regiment to go fight in Europe. Mike actually took the train to Prescott to put something together, but most the men of fighting age with any interest in fighting had already signed up at the fort, so it was just old men available, and Mike said to forget it.

But there was a moment when he seemed his old self. He loves our two-year-old Michael Jr. and is a very good father to him, but his mood has been poor for some time, very down, and he's drinking a bit too much, a bit like the old days. He continues to feel guilty about shipping arms on the Lusitania, though his was but a small part of that arms shipment.

Anyway, I tell you that as something of an explanation for the fact that he has signed up and will be doing firearms training of U.S. troops in England. I'm sure he will try to look you up when he can.

Now, Elsie, you know he has always been fond of you, and I think you of him. Wartime can be very romantic, so I'm asking you as a friend to keep things on the up and up, as I'm sure you will. Encourage him to stay off the drink and it will be easier.

But here's another bit of news: While I'm not quite through with my residency here in Los Angeles, the Royal Hospital in Chelsea, London, will take me on as a doctor, on account of the fact that wounded soldiers are already too much for England's hospitals to handle, and my knowledge of the new x-ray camera is much in demand.

My father and aunt will look after Michael Jr for the two or three months I'm away—the war is not expected to last much longer than that. Oh, and two of Mike's six sisters are in Los Angeles and want a share of Michael, Jr., too!

So, I will be able to see Mike and, with any luck, you as well! I would not be surprised if Robert Davies turns up there, based on a few things he hinted at about maybe seeing you soon.

All my love,
Antonia

A Place for Our Rain

234